*Sam refused to fall under his spell, but curiosity overcame her.*

She waved her hand for him to continue, hoping the carefully orchestrated gesture looked as careless as she wanted it to. Because she didn't care a whit about him.

She wouldn't. She *couldn't.*

Nic pursed his lips and nodded slightly, dislodging a lock of hair that fell over his forehead. He ruthlessly raked it back into place. But it was too late. She'd seen a vulnerability in his expression she'd never have thought he could feel.

"So… What I wanted to say…" He took a breath. "I was out of line…and I sincerely want to apologize."

Sam blinked. Of all the things she expected him to say, this was not one of them.

Dear Reader,

This is my second Hopewell Winery book, a series inspired by a real town in Pennsylvania and the origins of a real winery. Two immigrant brothers were given a vision of the future when they found a place that reminded them of their homeland, and in turn they inspired me. As I stood on the cliffs overlooking row after row of grapevines and, far below, the Schuylkill River, it all became clear. The brothers became sisters and two morphed into three. Then came the layers. I added to their pasts a series of events that changed each character in different ways, with the importance of family running through all the books as a central theme.

*A Bargain Called Marriage* explores the effects of both good and bad parenting in middle sister Samantha, the tomboy heroine, and Niccolò, the playboy, daredevil hero, and the road they travel to finding love in each others arms. Opposites are supposed to attract, but no one ever talks about the fireworks when they do.

Enjoy,

*Kate Welsh*

# A BARGAIN
# CALLED
# MARRIAGE

## *KATE WELSH*

# SPECIAL EDITION®
### Published by Silhouette Books
#### America's Publisher of Contemporary Romance

SILHOUETTE BOOKS

ISBN-13: 978-0-373-24839-1
ISBN-10:    0-373-24839-3

A BARGAIN CALLED MARRIAGE

Visit Silhouette Books at www.eHarlequin.com

Printed in U.S.A.

**Books by Kate Welsh**

Silhouette Special Edition

*The Doctor's Secret Child* #1734
*A Bargain Called Marriage* #1839

Love Inspired

*For the Sake of Her Child* #39
*Never Lie to an Angel* #69
*A Family for Christmas* #83
*Small-Town Dreams* #100
*Their Forever Love* #120
*\*The Girl Next Door* #156
*\*Silver Lining* #173
*\*Mountain Laurel* #187

*\*Her Perfect Match* #196
*Home to Safe Harbor* #213
*\*A Love Beyond* #218
*\*Abiding Love* #252
*\*Autumn Promises* #265
*Redeeming Travis* #271
*Joy in His Heart* #325

*Laurel Glen

## KATE WELSH

is a two-time winner of Romance Writers of America's coveted Golden Heart Award and was a finalist for RWA's RITA® Award in 1999. Kate lives in Havertown, Pennsylvania, with her husband of over thirty years. When not at work in her home office, creating stories and the characters that populate them, Kate fills her time in other creative outlets. There are few crafts she hasn't tried at least once or a sewing project that hasn't been a delicious temptation. Those ideas she can't resist grace her home or those of friends and family.

As a child she often lost herself in creating make-believe worlds and happily-ever-after tales. Kate turned back to creating happy endings when her husband challenged her to write down the stories in her head.

This book is dedicated to Debbie, sister-in-law by relationship—friend by heart. Thanks for sharing my love of wineries and poking through antique stores. Thanks for navigating on that special day when we hunted for this special winery. Lastly, thanks for listening to me plot this series the whole way home and for all the return trips since.

## Prologue

The bridal bouquet she'd planned to avoid even touching smacked Samantha Hopewell in the chest. She snapped her gaze upward to the balcony where her sister, Caroline, stood with her new husband. Then Sam looked back down at the bunch of flowers where they hung, stuck fast to the lacy bodice of her pale blue bridesmaid's gown. Not much of a choice. She either grabbed the handle and yanked it loose, or let it hang there looking like the biggest and most misplaced corsage in history. Since the latter would make her look like a fool, she took hold of the hated thing and pulled, sealing her supposed fate as the next bride.

As everyone around her complained of nepotism, Sam glanced back at the stairs leading to the balcony.

Her sister, who had turned adoring eyes on her new husband, stood on the step just below him. His devilish grin told Sam the other women at the reception had been right. The fix had been in and it had been Trey's idea. It was a good thing she wasn't superstitious about the curse surrounding the catching a bridal bouquet and being the next bride or she'd make Caro a widow before she was truly a bride.

Sam grinned up at the two of them, her sense of the ridiculous tickled. Everyone knew she'd never trust a man with her heart. Men were fickle creatures who, on a whole, were incapable of being faithful. She could only hope her sister had found one of the rare breed able to pull it off. Sam had certainly never run across one she'd thought *she* could trust.

Up on the stairs, Trey let go of Caro and pulled the lacy bridal garter out of his breast pocket. His grin grew even more mischievous as he surveyed the crowd of men who'd gathered. Something in his eyes had Sam's smile fading toward a frown.

Paybacks, his expression seemed to say, are a bitch.

And then he aimed the garter, with all the care and accuracy of a champion archer, right at the wild, daredevil playboy standing outside the group of eager men by the stairs.

Sam had only met Niccolò Verdini, her mother's godson, the night before, but she'd have mistrusted him on sight even if she hadn't spent years reading of his exploits. He was everything she loathed about men. Shallow. Macho. Careless. The thought of one of the world's foremost womanizers walking down the aisle was even more ridiculous than the idea that she would. Her sense of humor kicked in once again, and she laughed at Niccolò's obvious discomfort as he gazed down in shock at the satin-and-lace garter in his hand.

Niccolò had the lacy bit of fluff in his hand before he knew what had hit him. Then he heard Samantha Hopewell's laughter fill in the silence that had suddenly descended. Since meeting her last evening, he'd found her obvious leap to judgment of him and his lifestyle quite irritating. The way he lived his life hurt no one, so who was she to judge him?

"I don't know what she's laughing at," the groom's brother snickered next to Niccolò.

"I believe she sees irony in your quaint American custom," he said as he twirled the circlet of lace on his rotating finger. "This means I am doomed to marry soon, no? She is positive I am quite unwilling to settle for one woman." He grinned widely. "She would be right, of course. Marriage is not in my plans."

Griffin nodded toward Samantha. "You think she plans to give any guy even a chance with her?"

"Ah, I see. She would be similarly doomed."

"Yeah, but I'm talking about right now. Did you see Trey take the garter off Caroline before they climbed the stairs?"

Nic nodded.

"Another quaint but not always honored custom," Griffin went on, "is that you—the catcher of the garter—get to put it on the leg of the woman who caught the bouquet. Usually how well the guy knows the woman dictates how high up it goes." He paused significantly. "But…"

Nic grinned, and he knew it was tinged with mischief. "Ah. And are we to honor this interesting tradition at this wedding?"

"I intend to make sure we do. Sam's been more than a little hostile to my brother. And while I know she had her reasons in the beginning, I see it as my duty to make her life just a little miserable for Trey's sake."

"In that case, Griffin Westerly, I place myself at your disposal. As a groom, your brother already has enough problems."

Nic watched the best man hop up on the stage where the band played. The younger man talked to the lead singer and took the microphone as the drummer performed a dramatic drumroll.

"Would the lucky two who caught the bouquet and garter please come up front?" Griffin called out.

Several laughing young women who'd flocked around Samantha pushed her forward. Nic followed, pretending ignorance lest she be forewarned that he was part of a conspiracy.

Then Westerly said, "Could we have a chair please?" He jumped back down off the stage as an older man pushed a chair forward. Griffin grabbed it and placed the chair into a bright spot of light at the front of the bandstand.

Nic stepped into the circle formed by interested guests.

"As the next lucky bride and groom," Griff went on, "it's time to practice for your own happy wedding night," he finished with a comic waggle of his eyebrows.

As Nic drew nearer, he heard Samantha mutter, "You're a dead man, Westerly, and you, too, Verdini, if you carry this too far."

Griffin ignored Samantha and showed—or rather strong-armed—her to the chair. Meanwhile, Nic pretended complete and utter confusion with the strange proceedings.

"Nic," Griff explained, "we'd like to see you practice for your own wedding night with that garter you just snagged."

"Ah," Nic said as if understanding at last what was expected of him. While kneeling at the feet of his godmother's prickly daughter wasn't exactly at the top of his list, Nic recognized that some things were worth the eventual payoff. Gamely, he dropped to one knee in front of her. Then the band started playing striptease music.

Nic caught the lighthearted mood of the crowd and grinned as Samantha lifted her foot. He looked at her for the first time that day. Really looked. Close up.

She was beautiful. Yesterday when they'd met she'd been dressed in a baggy T-shirt and jeans. He thought of an American expression he'd heard just recently. Zia Juliana somehow had managed to make a silk purse of a sow's ear.

Nic cupped the heel of Samantha's delicate sandaled foot, a large improvement over the work boots she'd worn last evening. As he ran his hand over her finely shaped arch, a becoming blush bloomed on her silky cheeks. Then, to his surprise, he felt a shiver run through her as if she, too, felt electricity arcing between them. He didn't have time to analyze the sizzle because shouts from the crowd caught and egged on his devilish side. He slipped the garter past her ankle, then caressed her calf on his way to her knee.

His exploration continued upward and his fingertips reached the delicate, soft flesh of Samantha's inner thigh. His body betrayed him with a shot of honest-to-God desire. It zinged through him, muddling his mind. Still, he couldn't ignore it or call it irritation as he had the night before.

Then she bent forward and whispered, "If that goes any higher, I promise to make you regret it."

Her breath on his ear alarmed him more than her threat because it felt much too good. Nothing surprised him more than when he turned his head and found her lips only an inch from his own. For reasons that had nothing to do with good sense and everything to do with curiosity and the adrenaline rush he got from danger, Nic kissed her there in front of God, his current companion and everyone else.

"Thank you for sharing this most interesting and pleasant of American traditions, cousin," he whispered. Then his rusty sense of self-preservation restored itself. Nic stood quickly and departed from the circle of wedding guests with a dramatic bow.

Samantha wasn't his cousin, of course. But that

didn't matter because neither was she his type, he told himself when he looked back and saw her stomping in the opposite direction. He gravitated toward tall, willowy and willing women such as his current *amor* and not short, voluptuous, prickly misanthropes such as Samantha Hopewell. Yet the urge to follow her, and to get to know her and what made her tick, was so strong he decided not to prolong his stay but to leave for his next race in the morning.

## Chapter One

Niccolò Verdini watched with appreciative eyes as Shanté Lincoln gathered his things together and put them in his suitcase. Her café au lait skin glowed against the crisp white of her nurse's uniform. The intricate weaving and beading in her hair fascinated him, too. The arrangement caught the light from the window and sparkled like a thousand jewels. Cleopatra would have been jealous of the lovely Shanté.

Nic grinned at her when she glanced his way, and a telltale blush warmed her cheeks. He liked women. He liked talking to them. He liked touching them, holding them and making love to them. He liked every variety, size and nationality. He just didn't trust them with more than the physical—the temporary.

Right then he wished he could trust one of the many women he knew. Because thinking about the future and the haunting memory of the boat accident—of those minutes when Jake and he had struggled to free him from the wreckage—scared him out of his mind. He could still remember with perfect clarity the moment he'd surrendered to the water surrounding him.

He'd fought it for what had felt like a lifetime, his lungs burning in desperate need of oxygen. He'd fought it not because he'd feared death, but because, as his life had flashed across his mind, he hadn't liked what he'd seen.

Frankly, there had been nothing of value to see. Just a tortured childhood, a university degree he had no intention of ever using and day after meaningless day he'd spent since he'd earned it. He'd left home to join a racing team so he could see the world and escape the strangling demands of his father. But the years spent since that day, living for the moment, now felt wasted. Maybe because he'd realized he would be leaving nothing of value behind.

Nic had been more than mildly surprised that all the hard living he'd done had added up to an empty, wasted life. And now that a quick-thinking rescue crew and two well-trained paramedics had handed him a second chance, all he saw ahead was more of the same.

"You all ready to go, Niccolò?" Shanté Lincoln, R.N., asked at his side, thankfully dragging him back from his dark thoughts.

Nic smiled at her, took her hand and kissed it. "I will miss you most of all, *cara*," he said quietly holding her gaze. "You have been a great comfort to me."

"You are such a player," she said with a chuckle.

"You wound me," Nic declared, grinning now. All through this last week she'd lightened his spirits with her streetwise spunk, her keen intelligence and her quick-witted repartee. He would truly miss her.

"Niccolò, you'll be flirting on your deathbed," said his *padrina,* his godmother, from the doorway.

Nic tilted his head and grinned at her. "I should hope so. It is my mission to brighten the day of each and every lovely lady I encounter in my lifetime."

Zia Juliana chuckled and walked the rest of the way into his room. He had not seen her in almost a year since her oldest daughter's wedding and she was as beautiful as ever. "We'll take it from here, dear," *Zia* told the nurse. "I have his instructions from the surgeon and his prescriptions. Is he ready to leave?"

"All set," Shanté said. "I just have to load Casanova here into a wheelchair and he'll be on his way. Bring your car around to the lobby and he's all yours at the curb."

"I left a friend waiting there with the van."

Shanté nodded. "Okay then. You work hard in therapy, and you'll be back behind the wheel—or whatever you call it—in no time. Why you'd want to go back for more of this I still don't get, but it's all on you now."

Nic nodded solemnly as her dark eyes stared into his. She knew about the times he woke reliving the crash. That same fear flooded his entire being now. He wasn't sure he wanted to return to racing or if he'd ever gain enough use of his arm to be able to control a craft again, but what else did he have? He had only his racing. Nic looked away and back to Zia Juliana, remembering one of the regrets he'd had as the seconds under the water ticked by. "I didn't ask before. I was afraid of the answer I suppose. How did *Nonna* take the news of the accident?"

Juliana and Shanté traded looks. "Exactly as you'd expect. Your grandmother had seen the news footage so she was frantic. Your father is concerned, too, but I imagine you don't want to hear about that."

Nic's mood darkened even more. "You are wise as well as beautiful. I hope I am not causing you too much of a problem by recuperating at Hopewell Manor."

"The subject is closed," Juliana said deliberately.

He sighed. "Make that beautiful and stubborn. And since I cannot convince you to let me leave on my own, perhaps we should get this torture over with and be on our way."

And it was torture. His muscles pulled on his injured shoulder when he moved his head even slightly. And the minor sprain to his ankle made maneuvering much more difficult and tiring. Between the pain medication he was still on and exhaustion, Nic slept the entire four-hour trip to Hopetown.

It was actually the sudden lack of motion that roused him. He yawned and peered out the window toward the sun as it dipped behind a profusion of leafy green trees and majestic pines. And there before him in the rosy, evening glow stood the beautiful brick and stone mansion that was Hopewell Manor.

When he'd first arrived there last summer for the wedding of Zia Juliana's oldest daughter, Caroline, Nic had been impressed by the home of his *padrina*. But not because it was one of the oldest or grandest homes he'd seen since arriving in America one year earlier. He was sure he'd been in one that was older and a few that were grander but none so warm and welcoming. Zia Juliana had imbued her home with a generous, homey spirit in spite of its many priceless antiques and its place on America's historical homes register.

"Here we are," Zia Juliana said when Will Reiger opened the driver-side door. The older man slid to the ground and walked around the front of the SUV to open both passenger doors.

"Zia Juliana, your home is wonderful," Nic said, planning to make one last bid for the independence he'd spent years attaining. "But my being here will most certainly be an imposition. It would be just as easy for me to stay at that quaint little hotel in Hopetown. Room service could see to my needs and you could visit me once or twice a week. Everything I need would be close at hand and you would have no need to fuss over me."

Juliana stepped out of the vehicle and faced him, her gaze sharpening. "Are you trying to insult me?"

Nic felt his face heat. Abby, the youngest daughter, had told him on the phone that her mother could be formidable and now he saw she had been right. "No. Of course not. But—"

"But nothing. You don't like it when I fuss over you?"

"Of course I do. It is not that. I have no wish to be a bother to your whole family."

"You're my godson. You *are* family. Not by blood,

but by heart. Because of distance and circumstances, I was never able to be there for you as I should have been after your mother was killed. Now I can do more than write letters. And I'd like to think our home will offer what a hotel can't. Love. Family. I know that family means little to you other than your grandmother but, at Hopewell Manor, family is everything."

From the letters he'd received over the years from Zia Juliana, Nic knew that was true. As if on instinct, Nic sought what he had never had, the comfort of family warmth. He found himself easing out of the van to the ground and painfully following his godmother to a side entrance of welcoming Hopewell Manor. Though his head swam and his shoulder and arm throbbed, a feeling of peace enveloped him as they entered a large kitchen. There was a welcoming, Tuscan flair to the room that reminded him of *Nonna* and her home.

*Maybe here* family *means more than being controlled, belittled and badgered.*

From somewhere within the house came the delighted squeal of a child. Then, still laughing, the whirling dervish named Jamie tore through the foyer at the end of the hall leading out of the kitchen. His footsteps thundered upward on the sweeping staircase. Nic followed Juliana into the elegant foyer just as Samantha, the diminutive firebrand he'd tangled with at the wedding, arrived there in hot pursuit of her nephew.

"Jamie, I'm not kidding around here. Give it back! You had yours. I'm gonna catch up to you sooner or later. If you took even a bite— Oh!"

A teasing grin frozen on her lips, Samantha's captivating hazel eyes widened and she stopped dead when she saw them standing at the entrance to the foyer. Her gaze ping-ponged from him to her mother. Her cheeks were flushed and strands of her sun-kissed, wheat-colored hair escaped a tight ponytail at the back of her head.

"Mama, you're back!" She took a deep breath. "Abby and I made up the blue room for Niccolò. I know the bedroom's smaller, but that room has the private bath with the shower stall and the sitting room. Trey was home early so he ran cable to a television in there." She paused and brushed at the hair falling onto her cheek. "Oh, and we changed the linens to make the rooms more masculine." She paused in her discourse, her gaze avoiding Nic's. "Well, actually, Abby did the decorating stuff," she added with a self-deprecating chuckle. "I was just the muscle until Trey showed up. We knew you wanted Niccolò to feel welcome."

*Because as far as you are concerned, I'm not welcome here at all.*

Nic had no illusions about her opinion of him. He'd heard that loud and clear, though she'd sounded perfectly pleasant about the arrangements she and her sister had made in their mother's absence. Still, he knew Samantha was furious that he'd invaded her home.

And that was all his fault.

Had he not had a good many glasses of the vineyard's excellent wine at the wedding reception last year, he might not have let Griffin Westerly talk him into that reverse striptease he'd performed on Samantha with the garter. The kiss he could blame on nothing but a shameful lack of self-control. Unfortunately, he had done what he had done and now he would have to live with the consequences of his actions. He had thought she would be over her pique by now, but that appeared not to be the case.

"I appreciate every bit of effort your arrangements for my stay have cost you," he said, hoping to charm her. "I apologize for any trouble my arrival caused and for the time you had to spend away from your work in the vineyard and at the winery."

Samantha narrowed her eyes as if trying to find something in what he'd said to be annoyed about. Then, as if giving up for he was not worth the effort, Samantha shrugged. "Whatever. Pardon me while I track down my property."

"Jamie!" she shouted in no particular direction whatsoever. "That candy bar better be intact when I catch up to you." Her voice faded as she turned out of the foyer and down the hall he'd just limped along.

"I apologize, Niccolò. Samantha is—" his godmother began.

Nic held up his hand. "One of a kind," he quipped and realized it was true as a helpless smile took over his lips. He finally understood his attraction to someone so different from the women of his acquaintance. It wasn't attraction, per se. It was…curiosity. She was so different from the women he'd known that he could scarcely imagine what made her tick. He nearly sighed aloud in relief. Curiosity was so much safer than attraction, considering his connection to her mother.

Sam left her giggling nephew with a smile on her face although a bite was missing from her favorite chocolate bar. In truth, she'd never get angry at Jamie over something so unimportant. Jamie was special to her. He was her touchstone. Nearly her only happiness in an otherwise empty life.

She shook her head, banishing that foolish notion. She had plenty else to be thankful for—her mother and her sisters and her grapes. That should be enough for anyone. It was just that Niccolò somehow made her feel her life was inadequate. She was relieved that he had arrived now, while Jamie, Caro and Trey were still living at Hopewell Manor while a builder finished their new house. Their continued presence might make the house a bit more crowded, but Caro's family would certainly provide enough interference that Sam didn't have to worry much about being caught alone in the room with Niccolò.

Not that she was afraid of being alone with him or anything like that. It was just that—besides making her life look barren next to his—he also made her uncomfortably aware of physical needs she'd never had reason to acknowledge.

And then there'd been that moment. That awful moment a week and a half ago when he'd made her feel unexplained terror. They'd all been gathered in the family room after dinner to watch the weather on the evening news. The dismal forecast was followed by an innocuous sports segment that began with the scores of a doubleheader played that day. The Phillies had shut out the Mets. Sam had turned away from the TV set to rib her brother-in-law, Trey, a born and raised New Yorker. And that's when *it* had happened.

Her mother's gasp drew everyone's attention back to the television as the sportscaster said, "Now, watch this slow-mo replay of the crash. Rayburn cuts Verdini off and then the Italian's boat catches the American's wake and goes airborne. Verdini's boat flips twice and part of his cockpit canopy flies off just before the boat lands upside down, pinning him underwater, apparently tangled in the wreckage. Forester, his teammate, frantically tries to free him, going back under the capsized craft, twice, but to no avail." The footage switched back to the announcer. "Four minutes later, rescuers were finally able to cut him loose and pull him onto the rescue chopper."

The announcer had gone on enthusiastically, saying, "Don't worry, though, you can't keep this guy down. The good news is that paramedics were able to resuscitate Verdini and it appears from early tests that he suffered no brain trauma. Twenty-nine-year-old Niccolò Verdini, who set this sport on its collective ear when he arrived in it, will live to race again. He's undergoing surgery to repair a badly fractured shoulder, torn rotator cuff and broken wrist as we speak, but this was as close a call as you can have with the grim reaper and live to talk about it. Verdini, known for his fearlessness, has never been in a wreck this severe. Leaving fans and the rest of his team with a question tonight. Will the Italian Dynamo recover enough to get back on the circuit? Or will he hang up his helmet and let Jake Forester lead the team and take the chances now that death came a-knockin'?"

"Damn!" Sam shook her head sharply, trying to banish the image—the play-by-play—that kept repeating itself like a tape loop in her head. The image of Niccolò, usually so full of life, being pulled limp and still aboard the rescue craft seemed to have burned itself into her brain. "The man must have a death wish," she muttered before charging off to her fields.

Now, *there* was something to worry about. Her grapes. So far, this growing season there had only been a handful of good days. The precious root structures of her vines were drowning in Hopewell's fertile soil because April's showers had been more like April's deluge, followed by May's almost daily downpour. There had already been two out of three days of rain in June and the forecast for the rest of June didn't look much better. And worse, the vines were practically shivering in the unseasonably cool damp wind that swept up the cliffs from the river below.

What kind of summer was this? They needed dry soil and good old hot Pennsylvania dog days of summer or her grapes would be worthless for wine. If they had to buy them on the open market, Hopewell's overhead would kill their profits. For a fledgling winery, that could spell the beginning of the end.

Another problem was that she had desperately needed an easy summer in the fields this year. She'd had a pain-free year while on Lupron® but her time had run out. She'd had to go off the medication three months ago and her endometriosis had come back with a vengeance. All her abdominal functions were affected and she was in almost constant pain. Four surgeries before she'd gone on the medication had failed to help, so now she was out of options.

Except one. And that one would put an end to her ever being able to have children.

Well, that wasn't exactly the whole truth. She'd been given one option other than a hysterectomy and it might solve most of her problems. Pregnancy. She could get to have the baby she so desperately wanted and possibly feel better for it. The doctor said pregnancy could reduce her problem with endometriosis for up to five years. That was, if she managed to conceive.

Which led her to the next problem. She didn't date. So where was she supposed to find a father for her baby? Anonymous sex with a string of strangers was morally and personally abhorrent to her. And with all the STDs floating around, that solution could be even more dangerous for her health than her current problem. Or she could go to a fertility clinic and undergo artificial insemination, but Sam's medical insurance didn't cover that. Right now she couldn't handle the financial strain. But her objection to that method was more than monetary. To her, it felt wrong not to at least know her baby's father. She remembered seeing several mothers and their babies on a talk show. All eight were siblings sharing the same father. Sam didn't like the thought of the complications that could arise later for her child.

Sam's ability to deal with pain day in and day out had about run out, and she felt like a dishrag most mornings. She was out of time, left with no choice but to consider having the hysterectomy her gynecologist recommended.

Yet, that forever put an end to her dreams of motherhood.

Not for the first time Sam cursed her body. She felt like such a failure as a woman. Shaking her head, she banished her worries and got out of the pickup to finish her day's work. But her mind wouldn't stay off her troubling personal issues, even as she tied up the loose ends of her workday.

Walking among the vines on her way home, Sam wondered why she kept working so hard to save this legacy when it looked as if she'd have no one to pass it on to. That had been her mother's dream of Hopewell Winery for her daughters and it had quickly become Caro's, Abby's and Sam's, too. They'd all hoped that, on the plateau above the river, the four of them would build a legacy as rich and deep as the one Josiah Hopewell had started back in 1689 when he'd settled on the banks of the river far below.

For some unknown and truly quirky reason, thoughts of her dead-end future reminded her of Niccolò and those things he'd made her feel when he'd touched her at Caro's wedding. Not for the first time, she studiously banished any thought of him that crept into her mind. But those thoughts just didn't want to be silenced.

And that just wouldn't do!

An hour later, finally relaxed from a hot shower, Sam sneaked a peek into the parlor off the entrance foyer. It was blessedly deserted. The room still had a welcoming glow, even though it was slightly cast in shadows at this time of day—thanks to the huge oak trees that stood sentry on either corner of the front of the house.

Sam wandered into the golden parlor, skirted the sofa that sat with its high back toward the doorway. She dropped into one of the lemon-yellow, striped wingback chairs that bracketed the now dormant fireplace. With a tired sigh, Sam closed her eyes, letting her thoughts drift.

Something musky in the air reminded her of her precious fields again. In her mind's eye she saw the terraced terrain she'd just left. In spring, the vines sprouted delicate, pale-green shoots of renewed life. She moved her mental calendar forward and conjured up a vision of the vines blooming purple with delicate flowers dancing in the breeze as the sun rose warm, heating the air. In the next phase the vines hung heavy with fruit—a promise of the bounty to follow. Then seasonal workers, scattered across the fields, worked diligently to gather in a full, sweet harvest. After that the air would grow crisp and a golden hue would spread across the fields. The angle of the sun always changed dramatically after that as the bare, ocher-colored vines settled themselves for a long rejuvenating winter's sleep.

Maybe once the loss was fact, it wouldn't hurt so badly that she would have no child to pass all that beauty on to. She sighed, wishing that, like the vines in winter, she, too, could lose herself and her problems in a long restorative sleep.

"Hard day?" Niccolò's smooth baritone voice asked from just across from her.

Sam nearly jumped out of her skin. Hand flying to her thundering heart, she catapulted forward, sitting bolt upright. She stared for a long moment at Niccolò where he reclined on the long, overstuffed sofa. "You scared ten years off my life sneaking up on me like that," she charged.

"I apologize for startling you, but I didn't sneak anywhere. I believe it was you who failed to notice me. I was here when you came in. I took a few moments to study you before you could become annoyed by my presence. Then I realized my mistake since there seemed no way to tell you I was here without possibly startling you."

She refused to think about why he would watch her, nor would she care. "Why didn't you say anything before this?"

What looked like a sad smile tipped his full lips up a bit on the ends. "I had never seen you so still. I hated to disturb you. But then you looked troubled, and I felt responsible for some of that. The others will soon join us and my opportunity to speak with you alone will be gone."

"I can't imagine anything we have to talk about that couldn't be said in front of my family."

He winced a bit, a tinge of something she couldn't name reflected in his eyes. "There is. I have something I need to say and I need to say it without an audience, or I cannot avoid an embarrassing situation. I fear you may never give me the chance to be alone with you again no matter how long I stay here. I must take the opportunity to say this now."

She smirked and stood. "Would it surprise you to know you're absolutely right? Frankly, I don't want to spend one minute with you and I don't care what you find embarrassing. In fact, give me a minute to round up the rest of the family so I can make sure you're as embarrassed as possible."

Niccolò shook his head and reached an imploring hand toward her. "Please. It is not my feelings I seek to protect but yours. I deserve to feel embarrassed." He stared up at her, his dark bottomless eyes silently, but eloquently, begging for some form of understanding.

Sam refused to fall under his spell, but curiosity overcame her and she settled back in the chair. She waved her hand for him to continue, hoping the carefully orchestrated gesture looked as careless as she wanted it to. Because she didn't care a whit about him. She wouldn't. Couldn't.

Niccolò pursed his lips and nodded slightly, dislodging a lock of hair that fell over his forehead. He ruthlessly raked it back into place. But it was too late. She'd seen a vulnerability in his expression she'd never have thought he could feel. It made him a puzzle, and Sam had always been obsessed with puzzles.

"So… What I wanted to say…" He took a breath. "I was out of line at the wedding of your sister," he went on finally. "And for causing you to feel uncomfortable,

I sincerely want to apologize. I wish I could blame it on the influence of the wine or the company I'd been keeping, but that would be making excuses for my bad behavior. I would be forever grateful if you could find it in your heart to forgive me for being so crass."

Sam blinked. Of all the things she'd expected, this was not one of them. It would be small to deny his request, plus she didn't want him to think he'd made her feel anything other than outrage. She sat a bit straighter again. "First of all, you could easily have said that in front of everyone. As far as I'm concerned, the only people embarrassed were you and your date. I was raised to believe a gentleman would never have acted the way you did in public or treat a near stranger so shabbily. Therefore, the only thing you made me feel was anger. For what it's worth, though, I accept your apology."

Nic sighed, perhaps in relief—or maybe exasperation—because he couldn't charm her the way he did every other woman between eight and eighty. "To me, your forgiveness is worth a great deal. Truce?" he asked with a little grin, then he rolled a bit toward her and held out his hand.

Knowing he still had difficulty moving around because of the awkward angle his arm had been cast in, Sam stood and gave him her hand, thinking he meant to shake on their tentative cease-fire. "Truce," she said.

But instead of the quick handshake she'd expected, Niccolò Verdini, charming scoundrel and scum of the earth, ruined a simple bargain by kissing the back of her hand instead of shaking on their deal. At the touch of his cool lips on her skin, Sam's pulse skittered and took off at an alarming rate. Her stomach, too, did an unfamiliar sort of tango. How could he make her feel all these uncommon emotions?

*Because, clearly, I've lost my mind!*

Sam yanked her hand free of his, somehow managing to feel the scrape of the calluses on his hands. She ignored the frisson that skittered along her spine. "Don't waste your time pouring on the charm, Verdini. I'm not here to provide for your amusement just because you're bored without a woman hanging on your every word and giggling when you conjure up that sexy grin of yours. I said *truce,* not friends. A *truce* is a cease-fire."

One dark eyebrow arched. "You think my grin is sexy? I had no idea I have that effect on women."

"Yeah, right. Tell it to Miss Universe next time she's hanging all over you," she told him referring to a tabloid article she'd seen about him and last year's beauty queen.

"You have clearly never met her, or you would know it is not possible for her to think anything about anyone but herself and her reflection. Her ego is matched only by her…" He paused, his eyes sparkling with mischief before he grinned and added, "…Her tiara size."

He might have said tiara but his eyes said bra size. The man was despicable. "Okay. Let me make sure I have this straight. You replaced the one you brought to the wedding with Miss Universe, then you moved on to Barbie, the one who was crying on camera outside the hospital."

He frowned. "No. The woman at the hospital was named Monique. Not Barbie."

She let out an unladylike snort. "Believe me, she's nothing more than a walking, talking doll. Anyway, I hear *Monique* divested you of your wallet while you were in surgery. Nice class of people you hang out with."

"It was a small matter, and only its monetary content went missing."

"Mama was furious. Did you listen to her and press charges?"

Niccolò looked affronted. "Of course not. What Monique took was little more than the worth of a first-class ticket and several days at the hotel where we'd been staying. She was back in Europe before I realized anything was gone. It was hardly worth the bother of involving international authorities."

"Maybe you're a gentleman, after all."

He shook his head gravely. "Nothing so horrifying as that. I had no wish to find the details of our private matters splashed across the pages of the *Tattler* or the *Inquisitor.* You see, Monique would have retaliated rather nastily had I pressed charges."

She chuckled. "What a shame. That might have been interesting reading."

"Not for my grandmother. She is rather old-fashioned. She once told me there is a fine line between fame and infamy. I tread carefully near the line for her sake. Even now, I worry about how much this accident has once again thrust me into the crosshairs of publications such as those."

Sam and her family had tangled with notoriety years earlier. Her father, pillar of the community and descendant of Hopetown's founding family, had an illicit affair with his intern and a baby had resulted. When Juliana caught them together, it had been very public, very ugly and the talk of the town for months.

The mention of his grandmother's concern reminded Samantha of the film of Niccolò's accident. "If you're so worried about your *nonna*'s feelings, you should think about how she felt when she saw the footage of the crash?"

"That is why I wanted Zia Juliana to contact her and assure her that I was doing well and out of danger."

"I've heard a lot about your *nonna* over the years. I met her when we went to meet Mama's father a few years ago. She didn't strike me as a fool."

Niccolò looked affronted, his finely drawn eyebrows knitting together in a deep V. "Nonna is very sharp of mind. Very wise."

Sam shook her head, feeling her anger at him mount. Was he blind or just stupid? "Did you see that footage? You were dead, Niccolò. To quote a classic comedy sketch: You were no longer with us, you were headed for the Great Beyond, you'd rung down the final curtain and had all but joined the invisible choir!"

He flinched. "You have a cruel streak, Samantha," he said quietly.

"Whatever it takes, pal." Sam could see she'd struck some sort of nerve, but she wasn't backing down. She'd met his *nonna*. The woman deserved better than to spend her waning years worried for the life of her only grandson. Someone had to care enough to say these things and, barring that, someone had to have the guts to say it even if they couldn't abide being in the same room with him. She appeared to have been elected, not because she cared about him, she assured herself. It couldn't be that. She cared about her mother's elderly friend and she did have the guts to take him on. That was all there was to it.

And so, having assured herself that she wasn't the one who worried about him, she went on trying to wake him up to the reality of the way he lived his life.

"I heard your *nonna* crying on the phone to my mother. If you have a death wish, do a better job next time so you don't put the people who care about you through that kind of hell time and time again. If it's just that you're an adrenaline junkie, you'd better figure out damn quick that getting high on danger isn't good for your health unless you want a very short future. Your next accident may not kill you, but it may make you wish you were dead."

"Hello, children," her mother said as she floated regally into the room. "I see you're getting along famously, just like Punch and Judy."

"I was trying to tell Niccolò how upset you and his *nonna* were when they broadcast his little death scene in all its international gory glory."

"Goodness, Samantha, Niccolò didn't actually die. He's sitting right there. A bit the worse for wear, true, but very much alive."

"Which is more good luck than good management," Sam countered.

"Samantha has been lecturing me about my dangerous occupation and the wear and tear it puts on those who care about me. I believe I have worried your middle daughter greatly, Zia."

Sam crossed her arms and glared when he grinned. She wanted to smack that sexy grin right off his face. She was sure she'd almost gotten through. There'd been a glimmer of regret in his eyes for a few seconds before her mother had walked in. But then the charming, thoughtless rogue had returned with a vengeance.

"We were all concerned, Niccolò," Juliana continued, ever gracious. "How *is* your pain level now that you've had a chance to rest?"

Niccolò watched Sam's mother as she settled in the other wingback chair before answering. "It is kind of you to worry, but I'm fine. I don't wish to trouble you more than I already have." His eyes flicked back toward Sam and once again she saw a glimmer of some sort of deep-seated pain shadowing his eyes. It was a sorrow she didn't understand until he continued, reminding her he was estranged from his entire family but his *nonna*.

"Some would say I deserve the pain for worrying all of you. Some, like my sister, would be disappointed that the rescue helicopter reached me so quickly and that the paramedics performed their duties so well."

"Then, I'd say those people don't know how to care about another person," Juliana said pointedly.

Sam stared at her mother. Was she talking about Niccolò's family or Sam herself? Had she forgotten how to care? Had she lost that, along with her ability to trust? No. Though she was reluctant to admit it, she would care if Niccolò was hurt again. And she certainly hadn't wished him dead. As far as letting him know any of that, she was just cautious, and rightly so. What kind of fool would trust an international playboy with even a tiny piece of her heart?

## Chapter Two

Sam glanced carefully over her shoulder as she hurried across the vineyard complex. Yep. She was being followed by a particularly annoying society reporter for one of the big Philadelphia dailies. The woman had been hanging around the winery all day.

Niccolò had been there a week and word had obviously gotten out that he was there. In Sam's opinion, Pamela Jeffers was more gossip columnist than a reporter of true news—and it seemed she smelled a story about the infamous Niccolò Verdini. If Pamela got a story it would circle the world via the press services because Niccolò was international news.

And, if Sam wanted to keep from having her name

linked with his in every cheap rag that existed, then she was stuck hiding.

Why?

Because it was well known that Samantha Hopewell was the worst liar in two states. Maybe three. In junior high, she'd once been dumb enough to use the old the-dog-ate-my-homework excuse on her English teacher when everyone knew James Hopewell would never permit his children to have a dog—especially not one that was allowed in the house. And there was no way Pamela wouldn't see Sam's antagonism toward Niccolò and his wild lifestyle.

She might not be any good at prevarication but Sam was no fool. She knew why Pamela had chosen to run *her* to ground when her sisters were readily available. Why couldn't she go ask them probing questions? Abby was, as usual, at Cliff Walk Bed-and-Breakfast and Caro was in her office in the vineyard's main building. The reason was simple. Poison Pen Pamela knew a pigeon when she saw one. And if Sam said something that put the Hopewell name in the media in any way that was even slightly unflattering, Abby, the guard of the family honor, would cheerfully throttle her!

Just as Sam reached the doorway at the rear of the shop, she glanced back across the tasting room; sure enough, Pamela had opened the door to enter. Quickly stepping inside the entrance to the distilling room, Sam slid the door closed behind her. She had just released a quiet sigh of relief when she realized she'd made a tactical error.

Her mother's raised and angry voice echoed from the other side of the expansive room. Followed by Will Reiger's desperate one. "Juliana, you can't mean this!"

"Yes, I can. Go. Just pack your things and go!"

Sam winced, eyeing the door she'd just closed. It started to slide open. If she backtracked through the tasting room now, Poison Pamela would have her. Plus, if the reporter had been moving as quickly as Sam thought, then Pamela was probably the person at the door. After the embarrassment her father had caused her mother, Juliana didn't need or want notoriety thrust upon her again. Sam didn't want the reporter finding more of a "human-interest story" for her column than an international playboy recovering from a boat crash in the bucolic splendor of Hopewell Manor.

Her decision made, Sam quickly forced the door shut again and snicked the lock into place before breathing a sigh of relief. The door was soundproofed to mask the noise of machinery when it was running, so Sam was sure her mother and Will's argument would remain private. Well, as private as it could be with Sam trapped there and no way to sneak out another door!

Turning back toward her mother and Will, Sam saw Will move into the aisle and reach for Juliana. "Please listen."

"No. You lied to me and there's no excuse for it. You should have told me who your brother is. Who you are." Her mother's voice cracked like a whip in the damp air and Sam cringed, wishing she were anywhere else.

Sam understood only too well her mother's problem with lies, but Will was a good guy. There weren't many around, to be sure, but he was one of the few. He'd even told Sam and her sisters the truth more than two years ago. Will *was* a vintner but he'd left out that he was also half owner of Old Country Wines, a well-established and successful New York winery. He'd always been a silent partner with his half brother, but about ten years earlier he'd given up a successful career on Wall Street to join his brother and learn the wine business. The entire time he'd remained a silent partner so he could truly learn from the ground up. When he'd met Juliana seven years earlier, he'd quickly realized she didn't trust wealthy men so Will had pretended to only work for Old Country.

"I came here to help you build a new life as well as a winery because I love you," Will told Juliana.

"I barely knew you when you came here."

"Darlin', I think I loved you from the moment I saw you staring dreamily up at a stainless vat. I've spent seven years trying to get you to unlock the door to your heart—to open it and let me in. But all you're willing to do is open a window so I can watch you live your life without me. I'm not James Hopewell, but you can't see past him to see who I am."

"Apparently, I never knew you at all," Juliana countered.

The only sound for several long moments was equipment noises from outside. Then someone rolled the big doors at other the end of the cement block building closed. As the building darkened, so did the mood inside it.

"When are you going to see that it's safe to feel again, Jul? You know the saddest part of all this is that you've recognized the emptiness in your daughters' lives and you lament the way they've retreated from life. You've retreated, too, Juliana, but you can't see it. You encouraged Caroline's feelings for Trey, yet you've shut me out. I hadn't realized, till now, what a coward you are."

Sam frowned. *Was* her own life empty? Yesterday she'd felt as if it was. She'd always thought being single and guarding her heart was preferable to the chance of getting hurt as her mother had been by Sam's father. Did Will see her as a coward, too?

*Was* she a coward?

Sam faced the truth. She probably was.

But was she wrong?

Probably not.

She'd nearly reached the side door and possible escape when Will followed Juliana into the aisle next to the exit. Sam jumped back behind a steel kettle. Now there was no way she could get out that way. Backtracking through the tasting room wasn't an option, either, because someone was rattling the door from inside the shop. Sweat ran down Sam's spine in spite of the cool temperature.

Her mother was silent for a long time before saying, "It's you who's been the coward, keeping secrets and hiding your real agenda. Leave. Just get off my land. I'll have Trey pack up your room and ship your things."

Sam felt the edge of panic. What was her mother doing?

Will sounded even more desperate himself. "Don't let injured pride destroy all we've built between us. And for God's sake, don't do this to your business. To your daughter. You know Sammy isn't ready to carry the full responsibility for the wine or the grapes. Especially not this year!"

*I'll second that!* Samantha mentally shouted but she stayed rooted to the spot.

"I said go," Juliana said, her voice breaking a bit but still strong. Resolved. "You lied. I don't care what your intentions were or what you want to call it. I don't *care*," she said, a hint of tears in her voice now. Then quick footsteps from the other side of the steel kettle at her back told Sam her mother had fled the building through the door she herself had been hoping to use.

Someone opened the big doors at the other end of the building again just as Sam stepped around the kettle. The lowering sun cast Will's shadow long on the floor. He stood in the towering doorway, his head bent, staring at the ground. Then he shook his head and stalked off, his shadow melting away as he walked out of their lives.

Immobilized, Sam stared at the empty doorway feeling as if her world had just crumbled. What was she supposed to do now? Abject fear of the consequences of losing Will's expertise spurred her into action. She started to run after Will. He was right. She wasn't ready to fly solo as vintner or grower.

"Let him go," her mother called out, stopping Sam in her tracks.

Sam whirled back. She hadn't heard her mother return. It was apparent she hadn't come back to stop Will from leaving. "Mama, this is insane! He only kept quiet about who he is because you mistrust wealthy men. He just wanted a decent chance with you."

"You knew?" Juliana asked, then her green eyes widened. "All this time, you *knew?*"

Sam shook her head in denial. "We didn't know *all* the time he was here. He told us a while ago; he swore us to secrecy. We've been trying to get him to tell you. Will is the best thing that happened to us. We wouldn't be where we are without him."

Juliana threw her hands up. "I'll send him a thank-you card," she fumed. "Is there any other advice you have about my personal life?"

Samantha reached out and grabbed her mother's hand. "Mama, I'm sorry I was in here but I was trapped trying to avoid Pamela Jeffers. I couldn't go back the way I came or she'd have gotten an earful of your private business. I figured you'd rather have me hear your argument with Will than read about it in the paper."

Juliana nodded and turned away to a stack of labels lying on the table. Sam's mother appeared to have dismissed the importance of Sam's presence during the confrontation with Will, but her profile was stony as she sorted through the prototype labels she'd shown them all the night before. Though it didn't seem likely, Sam decided she had to try reasoning with Juliana. "Mama, this is about more than what's between you and Will. He was right. I'm not ready to take over. You know there are problems with all this rain and maybe with the fruit because of it."

Juliana shook her head. "We're on our own whether we're ready or not." She put her hand on Samantha's shoulder and squeezed. "You're just panicking. And for nothing. If you run into a problem, I'm sure Niccolò would be more than happy to help. He has a degree in viticulture and he worked around his family's winery practically his whole life. Still, I'm confident you'll do just fine on your own. Now, I have to run. I have a group waiting for a tour. Look through these and make a decision. I trust your opinion," she said, and smiled as she turned away.

The plastered-on smile didn't fool Sam. Her mother was deeply hurt because the love Will spoke of wasn't one-sided at all. But to admit that, Juliana would have to admit she had feelings for Will, and right then she was just too stubborn and angry.

Sam shook her head. She'd always wondered who she took after. Now she knew. She was every bit as stubborn as her mother. She'd be drawn and quartered before she'd ask that indolent wastrel Niccolò Verdini for the time of day, let alone advice. Being stubborn wasn't a bad thing, she assured herself. Grimacing, Sam headed back to work. Checking her vines would give her something else to think about.

Nic wandered to the window of the library and stared out at the river. He'd been told it usually flowed by at a slow pace, but right then it tumbled and surged as if out of control.

The perfect metaphor for his life of late.

He'd now been there at Hopewell Manor for two weeks and he felt ready to crawl out of his own skin. His shoulder ached. The incision itched. The cast keeping his wrist immobile was bulky, annoying and itched, as well. He tried to be thankful that his sore ankle had healed.

What he needed was something to do. Anything! Agitated as he was, Nic would even welcome the torture of his three-times-a-week therapy sessions. At least that would be proactive. He wouldn't feel as if he'd been hurtled toward an unknown place by some unseen force he had no control over.

He glanced back at the library table where he'd left the volume of depressing poetry he'd mistakenly begun reading. He'd read more in the weeks since his accident than he had in all the years since he left the university. He'd also been reading in English. About two days ago, he'd realized he was finally thinking in the tongue of the nation he hoped to make his new home. Why he'd chosen to read poetry today, he didn't know. His spirits were even lower than they'd been before he'd picked up the volume, and he hadn't thought that was possible.

Shaking his head, Nic returned his attention to the flawlessly manicured back lawn just outside the window and the dark roiling water beyond the grassy area.

"Good morning," Abigail Hopewell called out as she breezed into the room. "Or is it afternoon? Good Lord!"

she exclaimed softly as she lifted the book from the reading table where he'd been sitting. "Are you trying to depress yourself?" He heard her close the book and put it back on the shelf as he continued to stare at the river.

"It takes no effort at all to depress me right now."

"Then *The Ode to Melancholy* was certainly a poor choice. Keats was the most terminally melancholy of them all. He had tuberculosis and was dead by twenty-six, in case you didn't know," she teased. "If depression is your aim and you get to a place where you're seriously contemplating slitting your wrists, please try to remember that the rug in here is an antique. Mom will flip out if anything happens to it."

The indulgent smile in Abigail's voice made him feel slightly better. Abby was the most serene person he'd ever met. She was never too happy or too sad. Always tranquil and never overly emotional. She might not be as interesting as her older sister, but she was very restful to be around. He noticed that everyone seemed to tell her their troubles. He wondered why she didn't always look tired. It had to be extremely wearing to project a perfectly even temperament all the time. Especially when people insisted upon pouring their souls out to her.

Not wanting to add to her burden, though, Nic forced himself to smile at her when he turned around. "I shall keep the value of the rug in mind."

Her kind dark eyes made him forget his intention to leave her free of his troubles and Nic found himself being completely candid. "I was actually never all that interested in poetry but I'm about to climb the walls. I thought it would be calming. I failed to remember how depressing some poets can be until I found myself securely in the doldrums."

"I think your problem is you're bored and too polite to say so. I'm sure we seem, umm, *dull* compared to the people in your usual life."

He grimaced. "I don't wish to sound ungrateful. It's not the people. You have all been wonderful. It's just that I need to get out and about or…" He hesitated, searching for the right American phrase, then continued when it came to him, "I will lose my mind."

"It sounds as if the patient's going stir-crazy," Caroline said, striding into the room.

He wasn't sure what *stir* was, but *crazy* he related to very much right then.

"The patient has lost patience with us and our slow lifestyle," Abby teased.

"I believe I have lost patience with being so lazy, myself," he explained to both sisters. "I'm not used to sitting for long periods of time."

"You should come over to the winery with me," Caroline offered. "I just came by to pick up Jamie. Maybe you could keep an eye on him. He used to spend a lot more time there, but now that Will is gone…" She hesitated, frowned and then, on a sigh, said, "Will used to take Jamie with him to help with the grapes. It was mostly busywork, but it's a routine he misses. Sam's tried to fill in, but she's sort of overwhelmed right now."

"She is the one who took over the work of Will

Reiger? I was surprised when he left. A family problem, I understand? When is he due to return?"

Caroline looked at Abby and something passed between the sisters. "Uh…it doesn't look like he'll be back. Sam's in charge now. She was his assistant, and she's been learning from him what she didn't learn in college. So what do you say? My mom has a tasting and tour scheduled. You could tag along with the tour and get a feel for the operation."

He'd promised himself to stay away from their vineyard as much as possible, and he'd managed it for two long weeks. But he couldn't deny that he was intrigued by someone as young as Samantha taking over such a large responsibility so suddenly. Once again, he found himself drawn to something about her.

Not a good sign.

Ten minutes later Nic stepped up to the tasting counter at Bella Villa and lifted a glass of cabernet sauvignon. He swirled it about the glass with the ease of someone who had grown up with wine. While running the clear crisp ambrosia over his tongue, he listened as Zia Juliana explained some history of winemaking in Pennsylvania.

She told the group that William Penn had to be given credit for realizing that the region showed great promise for winemaking very early in its history. Penn even established his own vineyard on the banks of the Schuylkill River centuries before. She told them that the Central Delaware Valley was one of the few places in the world where cabernet sauvignon, pinot noir and Riesling grapes could be grown on the same vineyard. Hopewell Winery was one of those vineyards.

"We produced our first vintage four years after we planted fifty thousand plants that were cloned from European stock," Zia Juliana went on. "The family nursed the plants, pruning them back, burying them for the winter, uncovering them in spring. We did that until last year, when we felt they had grown accustomed to their environment."

After tasting several more varieties of wines from different vintage years, the tour moved into the naturally cool wine cellar. He learned their cellar was actually a cave that had been blasted thirty-five feet into the rocky hillside. Nic left the tour impressed by all the four women and Will Reiger had accomplished in so short a time.

As he strolled across the top of the plateau, he grew oddly homesick. The hilly area reminded him so much of home. He shook his head. That was ridiculous. He never longed for home!

Then his senses went on heightened alert when he saw Samantha on her knees below on the terraced hillside working at the base of the vines. It was just curiosity she made him feel, Nic told himself once again. Curiosity was not out of line.

Samantha Hopewell was an unusual woman who interested him the same way an experimental engine or new hull design would. Once again, she wore loose jeans and work boots. Along with a ball cap, one of her ever-present, oversized Hopewell Winery T-shirts completed what seemed to make up a uniform of a sort for her.

She shielded her eyes and looked up when he approached. He could have dismissed her if only he hadn't noticed how her green T-shirt turned her hazel eyes a smoky emerald. Instead, he was unable to look away. New experiences always tugged at him, he assured himself when he realized how hard it was to transfer his attention elsewhere.

Samantha was not the type of woman he was drawn to. *It's just the novelty of her,* he told himself. Getting to know her better would simply be a cure for his boredom—at least for today.

"I just finished your mother's VIP tour," he told Samantha.

She looked back to her work. "Staying buttoned up in the manor finally bored you, huh?"

"Not bored, exactly. I appreciate all your family has done for me since I came here," he replied. "Please don't misunderstand, but did you know there are two hundred and two books on top shelves in your library? On the second shelves from the top there are one hundred ninety—"

She held up a hand, her full cupid's-bow lip curling a bit. "I thought the idea with books is to read them, not count them."

Nic propped his free hand on his hip and grinned. She was a spitfire, which, he admitted to himself, he rather liked about her. "I thought we had effected a truce between us."

She nodded. "We did. I apologize if I sounded annoyed. I'm not at my best today."

He noticed then that she was a bit pale and drawn. "Anything I can help with?"

"Not unless you have a magic wand and a weather machine."

"No. If I did I would be a popular and wealthy man and certainly in demand by farmers worldwide."

She stood, mud clinging to her hands and the knees of her jeans. She didn't seem to notice, though something else seemed to make her grimace. She rotated her hips a bit as if trying to relieve a cramp.

"Nope. They'd never get the chance to hear about you. Once you'd arrived here, I'd have locked you and your magic machine in the wine cellar. We need all the help this year we can get."

"You worry for your grapes," he said. "I am concerned for my *padrina* and her family. This vineyard is so important to all of you." Perhaps most important to Samantha and Zia Juliana.

Samantha stared for a long moment and he could see so many emotions cross her expressive face that he got lost trying to decipher them. Then she spoke, and there was such discouragement in her tone that he forgot his ongoing analysis of her. "Yeah." There was a wealth of anxiety in the sigh that followed her simple admission. "I'm worried. I think botrytis is setting in."

The fungus could be a problem but it was sometimes an occurrence she could possibly turn to her advantage. "That is not necessarily a bad thing."

"Except we've never produced a sauterne style."

Her knowledge of the effect of botrytis made her skills grow in his estimation. Perhaps she was not so far beyond her ability with her new position.

"I just had an excellent Johannesburg Riesling at the tasting," he told her. "I understand in your first year here it was hot and dry. Zia Juliana said the vines in the Central Delaware Valley produce small clusters of grapes with big flavor. Your vintner used them to produce that excellent vintage. A few years ago an Australian friend of mine, who is also in the wine business, had a similar problem to the one you face this year. He labeled a dessert vintage Late Harvest Johannesburg Riesling. It did quite well for his vineyard. It was made from botrytis grapes. It had a honey, tropical fruit aroma. The acid and sweetness were in wonderful balance."

She looked intrigued and a bit less alarmed with her findings. After pulling off her hat and sticking it back on backward, she asked, "What did they recommend it be served with?"

He noticed how velvety her hazel eyes looked in the waning sunlight of the day. Then he realized she'd asked a question. He thought a moment. "I believe with most desserts or fresh fruit, sharp cheeses, oh, and chocolates, as well."

"So they sold it in half bottles and recommended smaller servings?"

"I believe so. Yes." Once again he was impressed by her knowledge. Will Reiger might no longer be needed as much as Nic had thought, except that Sam's workload must be exhausting.

"I guess that's one avenue to explore. Got any ideas that would stop that?" She gestured to the dark clouds approaching from the west.

"I wish I had that weather machine for you. Perhaps the dry weather your television weather person promised for the rest of the week will arrive and last long enough to be of help."

She nodded and once again yanked her hat off, then moved her ponytail about as if it were too tight. "A dry spell. From your lips to God's ears."

Nic grinned. "Although it makes learning to fit in here difficult, I love the way Americans take the phraseology of other cultures and make it part of your own language."

"That's us. Despite the bad press, we're still the great melting pot."

Nic gestured about them. "This is proof. You have a wonderful accomplishment here. You have taken the best of European knowledge and techniques and combined them with new and innovative ideas like using steel while aging. And you have succeeded."

"The stainless gives the wine a chance to keep more of the fruit's intensity. Will put us on to the idea."

"But I noticed you still finish in oak."

Her smile was gentle as she wiped her hands on her backside. "There's still a place for tradition. The oak helps add some complexity." She smirked. "French oak."

He shrugged. "Ah. We must give the French credit

for something other than champagne and retreating before their enemies."

She laughed and he felt dangerously happy to have caused her lightened mood. He wondered how long he might continue a civil conversation with her. "I saw the awards you took at the Amenti del Vino International Wine Competition this year. A gold, a silver and a bronze. Placing in three categories is very impressive. The pinot noir was some of the best I have tasted." He grinned, thinking he was glad Zia Juliana had insisted he recuperate here. "I am especially impressed and grateful since my father placed behind you all three times."

She frowned. "That doesn't make you feel disloyal?"

He shook his head. Perhaps she didn't know about his relationship—or lack of one—with his father. "Believe me, as I was growing up, Zia Juliana provided more moral support to me at a distance of thousands of miles through her letters than my father did from the next room."

She stepped forward and reached out. There was such total understanding in her eyes that it surprised him. Before he could respond someone called his name. It happened so fast he didn't have time to react. He looked left as a man with a camera jumped out from behind a row of grapevines and snapped several pictures before pivoting and dashing to a waiting car.

Samantha snatched her hand back as if burned, but he was sure it was too late. For that one moment, he was positive they'd looked as if they were engaged in an intimate conversation. In fact, they had been. "What was that all about?" she demanded.

Nic watched the car tear down the drive kicking up a plume of red dust. He shrugged. So went his life. "I heard of an American celebrity who once said there is no such thing as bad publicity," he replied absently. Nic was not entirely convinced that was correct when often the truth had little to do with what was printed in many tabloids. Still, he thought he should downplay the seriousness of it all. In the great scheme of things, someone else would be their next target within days.

"But I am not quite sure that's right," he admitted, and shrugged. He refused to let her know he was at all bothered by what the press said about him. He grinned and continued, "I imagine we will find out soon enough, though."

Her hazel-green eyes caught fire. "You mean, you think my name might be linked with yours in some supermarket rag? You may not care about your reputation since you don't have a good one to protect, but I do."

He'd like to say her poor opinion of him had no effect, but it did. Instead of lashing out as he might have in days gone by when dealing with his father or sister, he turned and walked away. Never again would he strike out in anger at someone, especially someone linked to what little family he had left.

"What are you going to do about this?" she shouted after him.

Nic stopped. Took a breath, pivoted to face her, still smiling. And he'd keep smiling even if it killed him! If she wanted to think the worst of him in every instance, it was her blood pressure climbing and not his. "Perhaps I plan to find out a little more about my latest lover."

## Chapter Three

Sam tossed a loaf of bread into her shopping cart, then a bottle of fabric softener. Next, she grabbed up some jelly off a sale shelf on her way to the deli section. After she snapped a number out of the dispenser, Sam anxiously prepared to wait her turn. Glancing nervously at her watch, she confirmed that it was nearly noon.

Not good. Not good at all.

She was supposed to have finished shopping before the twelve-to-eight shift came on. No chance of that now. Sam would never have volunteered to do these errands if she'd thought one delay after another would put her in the only grocery store in Hopewell at this time of the day. The plan had been to avoid Ron Johnson, the store manager. She certainly hadn't planned to put herself directly in his sights so he could needle her from his little office next to the deli the way he always did.

She wished she knew why he went out of his way to be obnoxious to her. She'd never done a thing to him but continually turn him down when he asked her out. And she'd done it in the nicest possible way even though he had a hard time taking no for an answer. She'd simply explained that she never dated and had no time for it anyway. Unfortunately, he'd taken her rejection personally. The last time she'd said no, he'd gone from wanting to spend time with her to wanting to score points off her on some invisible scoreboard.

Every time she ran into him, Sam honestly felt as if she'd been transported through time back to her high-school years. The whole thing was ridiculous and juvenile. And what was worse, it brought back all the bad memories of taunting classmates and made her feel more insecure than she could believe—than she should allow. She gripped the cart tighter, fighting anger.

Samantha Hopewell was a fully grown woman and an equal partner in a thriving business. Her wine had won international prizes. She stiffened her spine. She'd decided years ago to leave that insecure girl in the past where she belonged and she wouldn't become her again. She wouldn't!

"Well, look who it is. Sa-*man*-tha Hopewell," she heard from behind her.

Sam took a deep cleansing breath, determined not to let him see how much his attacks bothered her. No. She was determined not to let him bother her at all. She turned to face the raised, glass-enclosed office. "Hello, Ron," she replied in a wearied tone. "I may actually have to stop shopping here just to make sure your boring life gets even drearier."

"Nothing's dreary about life in the grocery biz, babe. Or in the wine biz, either, I hear. And to think I'd started to believe I was just the wrong gender for you. I didn't realize you were looking for an I-tal-ian man. Maybe if I'd told you my mother's maiden name is Romano, you'd have come out to play with me, too."

Okay, now she remembered why she'd have said no to Ron even if she were inclined toward dating. Ron Johnson was a jerk on his best day and everyone knew his mother was an O'Brien! "The only thing I want to see you play, Ron, is in traffic," she retorted. "The extra five miles to Grocery Mart will be worth not listening to you.

"I imagine we spend over a thousand dollars a month in here for the manor, not to mention the contracts for Bella Villa and Cliff Walk. And if you add in our employee spending—employees who all seem to like me and respect my opinions—I'd say you just screwed your career. Big-time. Especially after I call your corporate office and mention your sexual harassment and ethnic slurs as the reasons for the sudden drop in your sales figures."

Ron frowned deeply, looking shocked that she'd taken exception to his remark. He pointed to a tabloid page hanging on the outside wall of his cubicle. "Hey. I just repeated what I read."

He actually sounded worried. Good!

Then Sam followed his pointed finger with her eyes. She didn't know how she'd missed the picture. He'd hung the front page of the *Tattler* on the glass of his office. Walking to it, she stared at the photo and knew exactly the moment the picture had been taken. Five days earlier, she'd encountered Niccolò among the vines and they'd talked. Her mention of his father had upset him and she'd foolishly reached out to him.

In the resulting picture, he'd been standing a couple of feet in front of her but perspective made it look as if she not only had her hand on his shoulder but that she was plastered to his chest. Verdini Deserted by Fashion Model, read the headline. With a subheading, Cozies Up to Farm Girl.

Sam didn't have words for how angry she was. Not just at Ron, Niccolò and the paparazzi. She was furious at herself for the weak moment when she'd tried to comfort her mother's Lothario godson. Poor little rich boy with the mean daddy.

And she'd fallen for it!

She knew her eyes were blazing when she looked back up at Ron Johnson's supercilious expression. Without much thought at all, she ripped the article down, left her partially full cart where it stood, then stalked out of the small grocery store.

And the situation didn't get better as she tried to finish her errands. Mrs. Wells at the bakery asked how her new boyfriend was recovering from his injuries. Pastor Knolls from the Methodist church said he hoped she'd get Niccolò to the altar so he could make an honest woman of her! Sleazy businessman, Harley Bryant, mayor and bank president, urged her to hang on to the rich jock till she got the next balloon payment on the winery's mortgage out of him the way Caro did with Trey. Caroline had done nothing of the kind, of course. Trey had wanted to help Caro when she was several thousand dollars short on their payment—the fault of Bryant's machinations.

When she got her hands on Niccolò Verdini...

Nic heard the front door slam and a quick, thudding pace he knew was made by Samantha's boots on the hardwood leading out of the magnificent foyer and down the hall toward the kitchen. Then the sound of her voice reverberated off the walls and up the back stairs. "Mrs. Canton, where is that continental Casanova! I swear, I'll strangle him for this."

His suite of rooms was too far away from the kitchen to hear Hannah Canton answer Samantha, even though he always left the door to the upstairs hall standing open. It wasn't long, however, before he heard Samantha pelting up the back stairs and down the hall. He looked up as she stormed into his sitting room, her cheeks flushed and her hair escaping the rubber band confining it.

Nic didn't have to wonder long why her hazel eyes shot sparks. In her fist she held the crumpled front page of a tabloid. So the paparazzo had finally sold the pictures. Five days. The *Tattler* was slipping.

"Have you seen this?" she demanded.

Reaching out carefully, lest she take a chunk out of his hand, Nic took the crumpled piece of newsprint, smoothed it out and then read it. He understood why she was upset. He couldn't blame her, and he was almost sure she hadn't seen the inside spread such a cover denoted. But he had no control over what the press printed, nor was there anything he could do to stop their intrusions—or fix any problems they created. He'd learned early on that the more he protested a falsehood, the more people believed it. So he had adopted a detached attitude toward it all. It was either ignore it, or the stress would interfere with his concentration while preparing for a race. And that would be dangerous since he needed every bit of his attention on his boat and his competition when he was behind the wheel.

It would never do to let her know how much this whole reputation topic wore on him or how much he'd begun to long for the fantasy the photographer had created with his skillful framing of his subjects and his sneaky use of perspective. But, of course, that would be foolish, and Nic tried never to be foolish. He knew that he was no good at relationships and it was almost entirely his own fault. Instead of admitting anything, he took another moment to study the photo of them. "Hmm. A flattering shot of you. No?" he asked, reaching for a bored tone.

"The point is not whether the damn picture is flattering but that my picture is in there, at all," she countered through gritted teeth. "That my name is linked with yours, at all, for that matter! I never even looked at my face in that picture. I don't care what I look like."

Nic couldn't help it. He let his eyes drift down her body, then back up. "An obvious statement if ever there was one," he quipped, then was unable to hide a grin when her eyes widened and blazed with anger. He knew he was pushing her buttons, and even though it was a cliché of the greatest proportions, Samantha looked so alive when she was angry.

She narrowed her eyes and took a breath, clearly refusing to be baited further. "I didn't look at myself because I was too busy trying to figure out how I could have been so stupid as to feel sorry for you because your family is so screwed up. And all the while you just wanted to get back in the public eye any way you could. No such thing as bad publicity. Wasn't that what you said?"

Nic had known, as soon as he'd said it, that it would come back to haunt him. He never should have stooped to baiting her then or now. And as with his reputation with women, Nic had no one to thank for her anger but himself. He nodded, hoping that perhaps if he didn't try antagonizing her she would calm down.

"Samantha, will you please sit down?" he asked in his most reasonable tone, and was shocked nearly speechless when she dropped into the small settee across from him. It looked as if all the strength had just left her.

After a moment spent collecting his wits, Niccolò said, "I am sorry about the article." Then he went on trying to appease this middle daughter of his beloved *padrina*. "I assure you, I would never arrange such a thing and include the daughter of Zia Juliana in the scheme. I would never arrange such a thing for any reason. These things just happen to me because they have in the past. I am for them… I think the expression is *good press*. Most people know these stories are usually untrue. Consequently, they ignore them."

"Maybe in your circles they do, but I'm not so sure about mine. No less than half a dozen people I know made comments to me and most of them weren't flattering. Mama is going to hit the roof!"

"She will never believe such a thing. She will know I would never—"

"Niccolò," Hannah Canton called from the bottom of the back stairs. "You have a phone call from your grandmother."

*"Grazie,"* he called out, thanking Mrs. Canton. "Will you excuse me?" Nic said as he lifted the receiver. *"Nonna,"* he began, but got not another word said. His beloved grandmother launched at him with her full arsenal of guilt, threats and more for corrupting the daughter of her friend. He pulled the receiver from his ear and heard a snicker from Samantha as Nonna accused him of betraying Zia Juliana's trust and called him every name for swine and cad she had in her repertoire. When she said he had shamed her, he felt as if she'd driven a knife in his heart.

It was then that a miracle happened. Samantha took the receiver from his slack hand and quickly explained that once again the tabloids were playing false with the truth. In fluent Italian, she went on to tell Nonna that they were not involved with each other. Furthermore, they had managed very few civil words with each other since meeting.

That seemed to not only calm Nonna, but to fascinate her. She clearly believed it and, from what he heard of the conversation, Nonna began asking questions about him and then they proceeded to dissect his character. Soon they were laughing as if they were old friends.

Laughing.

At him.

While Nic was grateful Samantha had turned the tide of his formidable *nonna*'s anger, he found he was insulted by them making jokes at his expense and he was also vaguely worried by the camaraderie between them. After several minutes, Samantha placed the receiver down without even letting him talk to Nonna again.

Nic was hurt. "She did not wish to speak with me again?" he inquired.

Samantha stared at him as if he had grown another ear. "She said she'd call you again soon, but that she had a meeting to attend. She isn't angry with you anymore." But Samantha sounded very unsure of something. Her lovely eyes narrowed a bit in thought as she gazed at him for a moment longer. Then she blinked, as if returning from somewhere inside her quick mind. "Really. Don't worry. Everything's fine."

A weight lifted from his shoulders. "Ah. Well, then, I thank you for explaining the truth to her even if you both had much too much fun analyzing me."

Apparently, she had yet to finish with her dissection of his character, however. "Your *nonna* really is very important to you, isn't she?" Samantha asked.

Nic wasn't sure why he said it, but he told Samantha the absolute truth when he said, "She is the only woman I will ever love."

Sam didn't know why, but she found his statement so sad that she had to look away. There seemed to be more to him than she'd thought. It had taken her by surprise when Niccolò had looked so crushed when Dolores Verdini had said she was ashamed of him. Well, really, she'd shouted it. Sam could only conclude that he cared deeply for his grandmother and about her opinion of him. And so, Sam had reacted in the only way she'd thought right. She'd stepped in to straighten things out for him.

And then, when that was settled, he'd astounded her again with his bald statement. *She is the only woman I will ever love.*

Substitute *he* for *she* and *man* for *woman* and it was something Sam herself might have said of her father. But she had the feeling his *nonna* had been his refuge and not, as her father had been, a critic. At least, until his *nonna* called today. Unable to look at Niccolò, she stood and went to the window. Staring out, Sam didn't really see the view; she knew it by heart. She felt keenly that she needed to move the subject away from their mutual experiences and shared opinions, so she asked, "Is there anything we can do about the lies in the article?"

"Denying them would be a mistake," he replied flatly.

She turned and snapped, "Say what?"

Niccolò motioned with his hand in a dismissive gesture. "It only fuels speculation and prolongs attention. They keep trying to catch you in a lie." He lounged lazily in the chair, but Sam didn't think he was as relaxed as he appeared. Niccolò reminded her very much at that moment of a leopard, sitting in a tree, tail swinging indolently, but ever ready to leap if his prey got too close.

She realized he was most likely right about the tabloid press and human nature. Crestfallen, she nodded. Sam had hoped if he made a statement, his denial would be printed and everyone would know the truth. "I guess you'd know more about this than I do, but I hate being powerless. I just thought maybe you could threaten them with being sued for libel or something like that."

Niccolò shook his head, an expression of distaste on his face. "Libel is difficult to prove. The picture is not untrue. We *are* living under the same roof. We *were* talking that day. Even I believe you intended that touch as an expression of comfort when I told you how little I mean to my father. Also, I believe malice must be proved as the motive for the story. According to Nonna, the accompanying article is full of innuendo but never actually reaches any conclusion, nor is it an unflattering portrayal of either of us. It is an old game with them—this careful wording they hide behind."

"They tread a fine line just like you," she said quietly, and turned back to the window.

"Exactly. I have always seen it as a precarious game but this time there is a player not prepared to take part, and for that I apologize. I know this will make no sense, but I think the best thing to do is to be seen together platonically. Perhaps in Hopetown. That way, someone you know will most probably ask about the article and we will be given the chance to tell our side and word will reach the people you care about."

He wanted to be seen with her to convince people they weren't an item? "You're right. It makes no sense. None at all."

"Ah," he said, smiling again. "That is because you have no understanding of the way this works. Just as with denial, if you hide and shun the attention, they must pursue you. If you make yourself available to everyone and answer their questions, there is no secret the reporters can claim to reveal in their tabloids. You take away their story because anyone who asks questions can get answers. It gives them, at best, one column to write and then they find they must move on to another subject, another story that can be made into news."

Nic watched emotions play across Samantha's finely sculpted features. She had what he could only define as a sweetly innocent face when one got past the paradox of her salt-and-vinegar personality. Which left him wondering—not for the first time—what lay under her often brittle surface. He thought that perhaps a young woman didn't develop so impenetrable a shell unless there was a deep hurt involved. Considering her feelings toward men, he had to assume the injury had been delivered by a man. Though she was often difficult to deal with, he'd still like five minutes in a room with the man responsible. Men should hold good women in the highest esteem like the rare jewels they were.

"I have to go back into Hopetown," she said suddenly. "You could come along. I was so annoyed about that article I forgot some things and never made it to one store at all."

Nic waited a beat, trying to hide his surprise. "Excellent! That should afford us the perfect opportunity to get the true story out there. How long will it take you to get dressed for town?"

Samantha blinked, frowned, then glanced down at herself. She looked up. "What's wrong with how I'm dressed? I was just in town. Remember? Take it from me, the ag store doesn't require formal attire, nor do any of the other shops in town."

"No, of course not," he said, quickly having seen something in her eyes that was more deeply felt than her usual annoyance. Whatever he'd seen, she'd quickly covered it with sarcasm. "Forgive the continental expectations," he said, hoping to soothe her feelings. "One of the things I love about Americans is your informality. It's just that I have not yet become completely used to it. Am I overdressed for this excursion, then?"

She looked him up and down, taking in his blue oxford cloth shirt and cream-colored cotton trousers. He felt an annoying prickle of awareness as her gaze made its way back up from his feet.

*What is wrong with me?*

"You'll do," she replied after a long pause—a long uncomfortable pause, he had to admit.

Nic nodded and followed her down the stairs as she strode toward the front door. Samantha always seemed to be so full of barely leashed energy and running at full throttle. He was beginning to understand why. And that instinctive understanding of her bothered him even as he wondered what it was she was trying to outrun. He'd long since come to accept the truth of why he lived life, as they say, pedal to the metal. But seeing the same traits in one so innocent bothered him almost as much as his grasp of her feelings did.

He stopped on the front step and watched her for another moment. In spite of the below-average temperature, the damp, cool breeze that made his shoulder ache and the gray sky overhead, he had hope for the day. And that made no sense, either.

Nic caught up to Samantha at the Mercedes. It was Zia Juliana's vehicle but he'd seen each of the daughters drive it. If the keys were on the table in the foyer, it was the signal that the vehicle was available. He had a bit of trouble negotiating his entry to the low-slung front seat. His arm and shoulder screamed for attention every time he tilted his head at the wrong angle, and this time was no exception. He suffered in silence, refusing to let Samantha know she had him at so great a disadvantage. It took a bit of maneuvering, but he was soon seated next to her. When she didn't start the car, Nic glanced over to find her staring at him.

"We could have taken the pickup," she said, her expression earnest and open. "Why on earth didn't you say something? Or were you worried about damaging your hard-earned reputation as a jock and a stud?"

He tried to look unaffected by how close she came to the truth, but he quickly realized he was fighting a losing battle. Nic lived an illusion, the persona of a carefree speedboat racer and international playboy. It was a facade he'd carefully constructed and cultivated to keep a wall around his heart—to hide who he was so he couldn't be hurt. If he'd slept his way across Europe the way the tabloids had said, he would be too exhausted to walk, much less race.

That facade had worked well until now, and he was too tired to keep his guard up. Too tired to keep it up with this woman.

"I am almost glad you see the illusion for what it is, Samantha. I find I need a friend and just now I realize I have never really had a female friend other than Nonna."

Maybe it was his injury or his near death. But the simple fact was that he knew it was not necessary to hide his true self from Samantha. Like Nonna and Zia Juliana, she was one of the jewels. If there was one thing on earth he was absolutely positive of, it was that Samantha Hopewell had no designs on him. Not for his wealth and definitely not for his body.

And he refused to examine why that made him more than a bit sad.

## Chapter Four

There was something about Niccolò Sam couldn't help liking. Which annoyed her, since she was supposed to hate him. And even more disturbing, for the first time she could remember, she wished she were a different kind of woman. The kind an international playboy might look at twice.

The kind of woman she'd never wanted to be.

Narrowing her eyes, Sam examined what he'd said as she cranked the ignition, put the car in gear and started up the drive toward the road. He said she'd seen through his illusions.

What illusions?

Illusions were traits or objects that were other than what they appeared to be. But she hadn't seen past any aspect of his personality at all. Oh, she may have thought for a brief moment that she'd seen a glimpse of vulnerability, but she still wasn't sure that was even there. To her, he was still an adrenaline junkie and a womanizer.

She treated him the way she did because his counterfeit charm annoyed her. So, did he mean he wasn't what he appeared to be? And, further, was he saying he actually worked at keeping up his feckless appearance? "If it's all an illusion," she asked as she pulled out onto the winding road into town, "why squander your life on risky pursuits and shallow relationships?"

Niccolò dropped his head back against the headrest and laughed. "Maybe you should learn to express yourself more frankly," he told her, still smiling, then paused. He only continued after twisting carefully in the seat to face her. Sam felt his gaze settle on her and suppressed a shiver as a thrill traced up her spine.

"Perhaps I live the way I do," he was saying, "because I like the life I chose better than the one chosen for me by my father. As an American, you should appreciate a rebel spirit."

"Hmm." She bit her lip and weighed her words carefully. Was there a nice man behind the Casanova facade? Maybe she hadn't lost her mind. Maybe it was *that* man she'd sensed and had been attracted to all along. Maybe he showed the world a smoke screen to keep everyone at arm's length.

Whatever it was, she needed to solve the puzzle of Niccolò Verdini. "I wonder," she mused aloud, "are you as big a risk taker as you seem to be? Have you ever heard of a game called truth or dare?"

On a straight section of road now, she was able to glance at Niccolò to gauge his reaction. And she was gratified to see him look uncomfortable. "Truth or dare? I do not recall hearing of it."

"It goes like this—I ask you questions and you answer them truthfully."

He looked suspicious. "Or? Where does the dare come in?"

Hoping she'd read him correctly and that he wasn't just baiting her to amuse himself, she replied, "If you don't answer, you have to do anything I tell you to do."

"This sounds as if it could get dangerous, *cara,* for both of us." It came out like the purr of one of the big cats she'd seen at the zoo.

Sam thought she did a good job of repressing the shiver the timbre of his voice sent rocketing through her. And, she decided, she would ignore the innuendo in his tone, too. Because, unless she missed her guess, he'd been trying to distract her. Refusing to rise to the bait, Sam tilted her chin up a bit. "Friends are truthful with each other. Hiding who you are simply means you don't trust me and that you don't really want my friendship." To cut the seriousness of what she'd said, before he recognized her mission to solve the puzzle of exactly what kind a person he really was, she drawled, "Besides, are you saying you're afraid of little old me?"

Her false Southern accent drew a chuckle from Niccolò, lightening the moment as she'd hoped.

"I've learned never to underestimate a woman," he said, a bit under his breath. His reply still sounded just a tad too serious. Unfortunately, she'd just begun negotiating one of the many tight curves in the road so she couldn't look at him to see if his expression gave away any hint of his true feelings.

As she pulled to a stop at a one-lane bridge, Sam wondered what woman may have disappointed Niccolò. Another car was halfway across the narrow bridge so she waited patiently and took the moment to study his stunning profile as he gazed out the windshield lost in thought. When another car behind her honked, she dragged her gaze away and started her car forward again. Flustered, Sam forced her thoughts back to the subject at hand and off his near-perfect physical appearance.

Realizing where her thoughts had gone, she felt doubts arise. He wanted to be her friend? Could she handle even a limited friendship with her mother's godson? It just felt so dangerous and she wasn't one to take chances, especially where men were concerned. Will Reiger was actually the only male friend she'd ever had. Then she remembered overhearing Will's assessment of her. He thought all the Hopewell women were cowards except maybe Caro.

"Are you serious about wanting a friend?" she asked refusing to give in to fear.

"I rarely say things I don't mean. Not about important matters, at least. Friendship is perhaps the most important of all. It should not depend on the outcome of what sounds like a game for children."

She nodded, accepting his thoughts, but she was still uncomfortable with the mystery that surrounded his true nature. What kind of person was he really? "I suggested playing because my life's an open book. You know my mother came here after she married my father and that her family all but disowned her for it. You know my father betrayed Mama with the woman who became his second wife. You know he and his new wife died on his sailboat. I'm not sure if you were told that others died with them and that the accident was all my father's fault. Or that the estate was all but bankrupted by a lawsuit their families had filed."

"Zia Juliana wrote of all of this. And, of course, I knew her father called for her in his final months. I was gone from the vineyard by then, so I missed meeting her and all of her lovely daughters."

Sam pulled the car to a stop at a Stop sign and took another opportunity to glance at Niccolò. His dark eyes were trained on her—intent and assessing. Sam turned her head away and back on the road. "Niccolò, knock it off. Your saccharine compliments don't win you points with me."

Niccolò didn't respond so, as she moved her foot from brake to accelerator again, Sam took his silence for acceptance and returned to the subject of their lives and what they did and didn't know about each other. "All I know about you is what I've read in the newspaper clippings my mother collected since you started racing…and what I've accidentally seen on the covers of supermarket tabloids. All any of that told me was about races won and lost and your exploits with women."

"The ones I've won and lost, as well?" he asked, and she didn't need to look at him to know he was grinning that sexy Casanova grin of his. She'd heard it in his voice.

Once again she refused to rise to the bait. There was more to him than a string of women and races. He'd said as much. "Tell me about your family. Why did you refuse to go home after you were released from the hospital? Mama said you were worried about your *nonna*'s reaction to your accident and I know she was frantic about it. You must care about *her*, at least."

"Very much. Her worry over me is unfortunate but I have to be who I am. She understands this. I call her several times a week and I stop to see her whenever I'm near Florence. But I am most comfortable with a continent or an ocean between me and my father."

A man who cared about his grandmother but was at war with his father. Hmm. "What about your sister?" she asked.

"Aah. When you think sister, you probably picture someone a bit like Abigail or Caroline. Maybe a mix of the two. My sister, however, is a vindictive, manipulative witch with a poison personality and a shark of a lawyer for a husband."

Sam whistled and slowed to a stop at the first red light in the four-light town of Hopetown, Pennsylvania. She looked at him. At his tense jaw. His thinned lips. He wasn't the amiable, easygoing playboy now. The expression in his liquid chocolate eyes was stronger than anger. "What did your sister do to you that made you dislike her so intently?"

"Call it what it is. Hatred. Gina made my life miserable, probably from the day I was born. I cannot remember a day when tormenting me wasn't her sole purpose in life. She was angry and jealous because our father married my mother six months after her mother died."

"Well, they say women mourn and men replace," Sam said sarcastically, then realized she sounded as bitter and misanthropic as her brother-in-law had once accused her of being.

Niccolò's eyebrows rose but again he made no comment on her response. This time, though, she thought perhaps he hadn't noticed what she'd said because he seemed so wrapped up in his own thoughts. After a moment, he went on as if she hadn't spoken. "Perhaps, Gina had a right to be angry and resentful of my mother. Our father wanted a son to carry on the Verdini name at any cost—even Gina's feelings. My mother was the vessel and I was that son—the key to my father's immortality. He focused on me and only me, but it wasn't as if I'd asked for it, or as if I'd asked to be born, for that matter. Gina made life miserable for me until she married."

"Well, someone married her, so she can't be completely unlovable."

He snorted. "Actually, our father used her to bail him out of a bad business deal by arranging a marriage between Gina and a middle-aged, but wealthy, lawyer who'd promised to invest in Verdini Vineyards."

Sam was outraged. "He *sold* your sister?"

A dangerous grin shaped Niccolò's mouth. "I felt sorry for her for a while. I was twelve years old by then, so I knew about the intimacies of marriage. But believe me, it has turned out that the unhappy couple deserves each other." Niccolò pointed up ahead at the light. "Green means go here, too, no?"

She quickly looked away and turned down the street where a public parking lot sat next to a small park on the river. "I'm not sure anyone deserves to be married off like cattle, no matter how big a brat she was," Sam mused aloud, hoping to keep the conversation on track since he was letting her have a glimpse at his formative years.

"Gina protested at first, then Father pointed out how powerful the man was. He conceded that Bianco was fat, but he said he also smoked too much so he wouldn't be around all that long. He convinced her that not only would she gain a fine home and have a treasury worthy of a queen, there was also little doubt Bianco would die at an untimely age, leaving her a young, wealthy widow. Gina saw the light and was more than willing to comply. Nonna says they now have two miserably rotten children. They deserve *them,* too," he said with quiet satisfaction. "I take comfort in the knowledge that perhaps they get involved in all the mischief she once accused me of, which caused me grief with my father." He grinned. "And her husband was inspired by having a young wife. He quit smoking, lost weight and is now in wonderful health."

Sam fought a chuckle as she set the parking brake,

then turned in her seat to face Niccolò. "Did you ever try to look at life from Gina's point of view?"

Niccolò's grin faded, and he nodded. "I suppose it was almost natural for her to transfer her hatred and resentment of my mother to me after my mother walked out, but I was already terribly unhappy and an innocent. Then," he added, and the grin returned, but this time it was the grin of an unrepentant rogue. Once again, she decided he used it to distract people.

"Knock it off, Verdini," Sam snapped, annoyed because the grin made her stomach do a wild flip, even though she was nearly sure he was trying to divert her. She got out of the car to cover her reaction and walked around the hood to stand next to him. Exasperated as she was, Sam couldn't watch him struggle to get out of the passenger seat without offering to help. She silently braced the door so it couldn't fall back against his shoulder. All the while, she concentrated on figuring out why he worked so hard at trying to look like a bad seed.

"Why are you angry?" he asked, his dark eyes narrowed in confusion.

She looked up at him and met his gaze as boldly as she could. "Because we've already established that I don't buy the act."

He swallowed. "It is refreshing to have a woman see through the amiable facade to the cad beneath. But I confess it to be disturbing, as well."

She thought of Niccolò playing so gently with her nephew Jamie when he was out of sorts that morning after Caro and Trey left for a conference with their builder. And she remembered that he'd written to her mother all through the years when Juliana had been hungering for news from home. They were the years when teenagers usually shun writing, yet he had written faithfully to an adult he had never actually met. Juliana had been his godmother by proxy.

"Actually, that isn't the way I see you at all," she explained, and turned away to lead him over to a bench by the water. Once he'd settled there, she crossed her arms and looked down at him. "I think the cad is the facade, and it may just hide a very kindhearted man. I thought this was truth or dare we were playing. Which means you really have to tell the truth. You said your mother left. Did you ever get to see her again?"

He frowned and looked toward the water but he did answer. "No. When I was seven she left me behind and was killed in an accident weeks later." His voice had chilled to glacial proportions.

"I'm sorry," Sam said, and blinked back tears that were rooted in the scars a woman had left on the soul of her child, decades earlier. How could Niccolò affect her like this? She never cried! Then she thought about her own situation.

"I can't imagine what that would do to a child. It was bad enough losing my father as an adult with unresolved anger between us."

Niccolò shrugged carelessly and slid a bit lower on the bench. Sam remained standing, but leaned back against the railing along the river wall.

"It worked out well enough, I suppose," he said after a bit. "We moved into the main house and *Nonna* was wonderful to me. She stood up to my father more than my mother ever had."

"I got the idea from Mama that you don't see your father anymore?"

"No. After Nonno Emidio'd died, I'd helped *Nonna* find an apartment off a little piazza in Florence. *Nonno* had split his fortune four ways between her, my father, Gina and me. *Nonna* had been happy to leave the vineyard and return to her hometown."

There was something in Niccolò's eyes she couldn't help interpret as hurt. "Do you *want* to see your father?"

"I don't care to ever see him again, no. Nor does he care to see me." His voice was tight and strained.

"That bothers you, doesn't it?"

He shrugged but the gesture missed looking careless by a mile. "Only that I wish he had been a father who was willing to love me no matter what I chose to do with my life."

"I can understand any parent not wanting their child to risk his life the way you do."

"It was more than that. When I'd found my first sponsor, it was just after I'd graduated from the university. He was there when I'd gotten the call from Franco that he was willing to have me race with his team. I'd been ecstatic. Someone was willing to let me pilot a very expensive boat for him. To let me be part of something he'd built from the floor up. The man trusted me. *Me!*

"My father had turned his back and walked out the

door of the house and never spoke to me again, even when I visited my grandparents. Had he even tried to understand, I might have raced only part of the year and given the rest of my time to the vineyards. As it is, I race full-time and I've been a success. I have my own team now since *Nonno* left me part of the estate."

*I should file Niccolò's life story under, "Your life could have been worse, Samantha."*

She sighed quietly. Her father hadn't understood her, either. And while he'd been hard on her for her "unlady-like" ways, he hadn't turned his back on her. "Your father never changed his mind even though you've been successful?" she asked.

Niccolò shifted his weight to ease the pain in his neck and shoulder. He was no longer taking the pain-killers. They only seemed to deepen his depression, so a little discomfort seemed worth the exchange. His strength grew each day and he knew his wrist grew stronger inside the cast. If only he could mend the painful fractures of his childhood in a few weeks, the way nature healed his physical injuries.

But the pain of his early life lingered. It had transformed itself into this endless sting of anger and resentment against the mother who had failed to defend him or love him enough to take him away with her. Instead, she had left him with his father and nasty sister. His father had grown bitter because of her desertion and, in fact, seemed to get more resentful the more success Nic found away from him. Nic wished he could forget the pain of his childhood and of his father's rejection in quiet times the way he was able to forget while in the rush of a race.

"I'm sorry," Sam told him, and he could tell she meant it. "I didn't have the best relationship with my father, either," she went on. "He tended to belittle me when I didn't dress to suit him. He may have introduced me as his she-male daughter, but he never denied that I was his child."

Nic blinked. "I find that inexcusably cruel," he said. Perhaps this was the origin of her dogged determination to dress in the least flattering way she could. But, even so, Samantha was definitely all woman. Even in heavy work boots, she didn't clomp along, but moved with a fluid grace that could not be denied. Nor could the curvaceous form she hid under baggy jeans and oversized T-shirts. She wore her personal uniform like armor. He wondered if she feared her femininity, or just that men might notice it and her if she let it show.

He knew her well enough already, however, to know she was not ready to have him ask that particular question. Instead, he added, "Perhaps, we do have a basis for a friendship. We had parents who made mistakes, but we survived because of other wonderful people who tried to make up for their...their..."

"Shortcomings," she supplied when he hesitated over the right word in her language.

He nodded.

Smiling, Sam slapped her hands on her thighs and straightened. "Well, this has certainly turned into a pity party of gargantuan proportions. Why don't you rest here and I'll be back as soon as I can?"

Nic noticed she didn't agree or disagree with him about the possibility of their being friends. He couldn't say why he even cared. She truly was not his type. He fought a rueful grin. But then, none of his other friends were, either—male, all of them. Maybe he was just bored, but he was no longer sure this was about curiosity. If it was, he probably would give up on her at this point. He rarely put much energy into getting to know people, so he was a bit surprised to hear himself calling her name. When she turned back, he said, "I thought the reason I accompanied you was that we were to be seen together. Did I see a restaurant on that main road? Perhaps we could eat there to accomplish our goal. And I could buy you a meal to repay you for boring you with the sad story of my childhood."

He felt better when she looked just as surprised to be saying, "I'll call home and tell Hannah we won't be there for lunch. You'll love the French-fried sweet potatoes they serve at the Hopetown Inn. Give me half an hour to finish the errands and I'll be back to get you. Or would you rather come along now?"

Feeling strangely energized, Nic agreed to meet her at the restaurant. But, after she walked off leaving him to his thoughts, he felt a bit of panic. What would two people of such diverse interests and personalities possibly find to talk about over an entire meal—alone. Nic decided he had lost his mind, but still he stood to go explore the shops and make his way to the restaurant.

This was proving to be a more interesting day than he had been ready for. Boredom seemed much less dangerous than lunch with Samantha Hopewell. It was good that he had grown used to living dangerously.

## Chapter Five

The sidewalks weren't quite as crowded as they'd been on the weekend Nic had visited for Caroline's wedding. Perhaps it was the gray day or that it was the start of a workweek. Whatever the reason, Nic was glad there wasn't the crush of people roaming the streets today that there had been the last time.

He poked through a few shops, noticed a few raised eyebrows from shop owners over his presence, but no one was crass enough to ask about his supposed relationship with Samantha. After a while, he realized that, for the most part, the only locals in town were the people behind the counters, waiting tables or stocking shelves.

Nic walked through an art gallery with some surprisingly fine art pieces, reserving one of the winery for Zia

Juliana. It was painted looking uphill through the blooming vines at Bella Villa.

Across from the Hopetown Inn and its busy restaurant where he'd promised to meet Samantha, Nic noticed a shop that sold jewelry. The window had a display of very interesting, one-of-a-kind designs worthy of shops on the Rue de Faubourg St. Honoré or the Via Veneto. He strolled in to ask the price of one that was perfect for Nonna. It was an artistic rendering of a classic design that reminded him of the set Trey Westerly had given Caro for their wedding day.

"I'd think you'd be better off buying her an engagement ring, young man," the voice of an older woman said from behind Nic just as he was about to turn to leave after paying for and receiving his merchandise.

*"Perdono?"* he asked, incredulous as he stared down at a small raisin of a woman whose mouth was so puckered it looked as if she'd just tossed back a shot of dry vermouth. Then he realized that, as usual, when he was flustered, his native language had popped out.

"An engagement ring. From what I hear, you should be in the market for one. That bauble isn't going to rescue Samantha Hopewell's reputation, young man."

Nic tilted his head and stared at her for a long moment. The silence in the busy shop told its own story. Whatever he said would be all over town by morning. Small towns, he thought with an inward sigh. They appeared to be the same the world over. He'd thought in progressive and free America it would be different. Standing before this disapproving woman, Nic understood Samantha's anger about the tabloid article. And now he was angry, too. Why was it that, although small-town residents should know the character of the people raised in their midst, they seemed so ready to believe the worst of each other?

This woman should know Samantha well enough to know she'd never be involved in a casual affair. So, considering that, she should certainly have been discreet enough not to interfere in a serious relationship between a couple. Suppose he were a reluctant suitor and this woman scared him away with her out-of-all-proportion expectations.

"This is not for my friend, Samantha. It is for my *nonna*. I was…" He stopped searching for the right idiom, "window-shopping and knew it had to grace her beautiful neck."

"And what exactly is a *nonna?*" she demanded, clearly outraged and thinking the worst.

Nic smiled and glanced out the window. Samantha was across the street pacing, looking back and forth up and down Main Street. He had successfully maneuvered this woman exactly where he wanted her and now, hopefully, he would spring his trap and leave her dismayed at her own behavior. Frowning and trying to look confused, not elated, he asked, "*Nonna?* In your language *nonna* is grandmother. You object to a man buying a gift for his *nonna?*"

"Well, no, but—"

"If you will excuse me, there is my friend. You do know that her mother is my godmother, yes? We are to meet for luncheon," he said, gesturing out the window toward where Samantha stood across the street. Without another word, he stalked out and started across the narrow street. Samantha spotted him and smiled, but then her gaze shifted to the door he'd just exited. The woman, he imagined, still watched him from either the sidewalk or inside the store. Concern and embarrassment replaced Samantha's carefree expression immediately.

"What did Meryl Bryant have to say?" she wanted to know.

He turned and looked back. The woman had indeed exited the shop and stood unashamedly staring at them with her arms crossed in a belligerent stance. He noticed he couldn't see inside the jewelry store. For Samantha to make an assumption like that the woman must have a reputation for intruding into business not her own. "How did you know we spoke?"

Samantha looked at him askance. "She wouldn't pass up an opportunity to stick her nose in someone else's business. She's the town busybody."

Nic laughed. "Busybody? Americans have such an interesting turn of phrase."

"So what did she say?"

"I believe she was outraged that I would buy Nonna a necklace and not an engagement ring for you."

"Oh, good, sweet Lord! What is wrong with that woman? I'm sorry, Niccolò."

It angered Nic to see Samantha so acutely embarrassed. "Think nothing of it," he told her, waving away her concern. He took her elbow. "Come. We will eat, enjoy this beautiful day, these wonderful sweet fries you spoke of and each other's company."

Samantha didn't look as if he'd be able to distract her. "Niccolò, the day stinks. It's ten degrees below average, the sun is a no-show, yet again, and it's starting to spit."

He looked up at the dismal sky, then shrugged without thinking. And his shoulder sent a shot of pain arching through his back and neck and down his arm. Instead of looking careless as he'd meant to, he let out a yelp of pain before he could hold it in.

Samantha glanced his way. "And, because of that, I made reservations for the inside dining room. I was afraid this damp breeze was going to play havoc with your shoulder. And I see it is."

"It was my own fault. If you wish to sit out here and watch the tourists roam the town, I wouldn't—"

"Niccolò," Sam interrupted holding up her hand. "Your shoulder pain aside, I'm not exactly in the mood to sit out here watching it drizzle. I won't enjoy my meal when every drop of rain reminds me that, even with over ten thousand feet of drainage, my grapes are drowning up at the vineyard."

"Inside will be fine, in that case."

Samantha nodded and they walked up the stairs toward the hostess station up ahead. A rather plain-looking, tall woman stood at an antique lectern looking over a list of names. She had carrot-red hair and a great many freckles. But, plain as she was, her friendly smile when she noticed Samantha transformed her face. There was a kindness to it that spoke of a good soul and negated any plainness about her.

She looked from Samantha to him and then back again. "Samantha. Hi," she said hesitantly.

"Jean Anne. You're back at work. I'm glad you're feeling better. How are Jerry and Sue?"

"Growing like weeds. Are you thinking about having the kids' camp again this August?"

Samantha shrugged. "I haven't decided. To tell you the truth, I wasn't sure if the kids had fun."

"Mine sure did. They did nothing for weeks but work on convincing us to build a grape arbor so they could plant grapevines to grow on it. We decided to go along with them. They had a blast teaching us all you'd taught them. It gave them such a wonderful sense of accomplishment. Please think about doing it again. It was a great experience for them."

Samantha nodded. "I'll give it some more thought. I'm a little tight on time this summer, though."

The hostess picked up two menus and moved toward the doors to the inside dinning room. "I heard Will Reiger left, so I guess you are busy. I'll tell the kids it's only a maybe. By the way, Jerry Senior's cooking this afternoon." She winked. "Think about the crab cakes. Nonsmoking, right?"

Glancing back at him, Samantha said, "I reserved a table inside and it's nonsmoking. I hope that's okay, Niccolò?"

"Nonsmoking is fine." He grinned. "I have given it up for my health. Far too dangerous."

Sam snorted. "Right. And you wouldn't want to live dangerously, now, would you?"

"Of course not," he readily agreed, but kept his expression teasing. He had begun to feel differently about racing. He'd begun to rethink risking his life for prize money and the glory of yet another trophy of dubious value to the rest of the world. But he didn't know what that would mean for his future, so he wasn't yet ready to announce any changes to his lifestyle.

"You're ridiculous, you know that?" she said, laughing as the hostess placed the menus on a table in a quiet corner.

"Have a nice meal, you two," Sam's friend told them. "Your waitress should be along for your drink orders in a few minutes." Her blue eyes sparkled with mischief. "We carry a rather nice cab-sav from an up-and-coming local winery. You might enjoy it with the crab cakes."

"I'll be sure to give it a try," Samantha agreed.

Nic frowned. "I am insulted that you would call me ridiculous when it is you who just agreed to buy a competitor's product," he said once the hostess had walked away.

Samantha shook her head and laughed. "It would be if we didn't supply Jean Anne and Jerry with all their house wines and several of their premium selections."

"It's good to hear you laugh, even if at my expense." In truth, Nic didn't mind being laughed at if he managed to lighten Samantha's mood a bit. She seemed always to be on edge, worried, sad even.

She leaned closer. "If you keep saying things like that, you're going to confirm that *Tattler* article, not refute it."

"Nonsense. We are here for two reasons. One is to tell your acquaintances we are only friends, and the other is to actually become friends."

"Okay, friend. My life is still an open book as far as I can see. What was it you wanted to know about me?"

"Tell me about this camping you do with children."

She shook her head, her golden ponytail bobbing about behind her. "Not camping. Camp. Camp is like a retreat, a minivacation, but for children without their parents being included. I had some local kids come up to the vineyard and help start a new section last summer. I'm not sure who had more fun, them or me. I know who got dirtier."

"Did your nephew join in?"

"He did. It was actually a breakthrough for him." She grinned happily, the green wedges in her hazel eyes sparkled. "He was the dirtiest. And bath time wasn't as bad as it had been before that. He was always so careful while he helped Will, it used to make me want to cry. He's made great strides since Trey and Caro got married. By the way, I wanted to thank you for what you did today. I know you were in no mood to play Chinese checkers with an eight-year-old. It really helped take Jamie's mind off not being able to go with Caro and Trey to the building site."

"It is nice to see how your whole family pitches in with him. With the Hopewell women, family means a great deal, no? I enjoy seeing the way everyone in your family cares so much for each other."

"Even though you're bored silly being stuck here in the sticks with us?"

Nic frowned. He prided himself on his good English, but, at times, Americans were just not understandable. "I am a bit depressed, I think, Samantha. Not silly. I miss activity."

She giggled. It wasn't a mere chuckle or polite burst of laughter. It was a carefree giggle that erupted and appeared to surprise her so much she covered her mouth to stifle it. She looked into her lap, trying to stifle herself.

"I have apparently amused you so, perhaps, I *am* silly," he said, glad to hear her sound so lighthearted but not sure if he liked looking foolish enough to elicit such a response.

Sam got herself under control and looked up. Though he'd sounded annoyed, there was merriment in his eyes. "*Bored silly* means bored to the point of madness," she explained.

"Ah!" Nic laughed before adding, "That is what I am, then. And *sticks?* What is *sticks?*"

"The *sticks* means being out in the country where people aren't usually as sophisticated as in the cities or high-end suburbs. And, before you ask, I don't know where it comes from. Maybe because in the winter we're surrounded with what looks like sticks when most of the trees and underbrush go dormant."

"I grew up in the country, Samantha," Niccolò explained. "It is what I was accustomed to until I turned to racing. I find it restful here and not boring. It is the inactivity that wears on me." He picked up his menu. "So where are these fries you recommend? If I am to flirt with the waitress to show everyone I am not involved with you, we must be ready to order."

Sam hadn't thought of that as part of the solution to the article and worried that the waitress would get hurt, but Niccolò was a master. He had young Becky Brady blushing and smiling and paying extra attention to their table. Still, there was no way the young girl could have misunderstood that this was just Niccolò being Niccolò and that there was nothing personal in his attention to her.

Niccolò chatted through lunch with Sam and laughed often about his occasional confusion over the many idioms that were part of the language in the United States. Generally, they just got to know one another. For Sam, that was a double-edged sword—speaking of idioms.

Nic was funny and kind and, unlike her handsome father, took people at face value. In fact, Niccolò seemed able to look past even a face. He even mentioned how Jean Anne's beauty shone when she smiled. All through school, Jean Anne had been the beanpole with too many freckles whom Sam had tried to protect from nasty classmates.

When Sam paired his kindness and his sense of humor with the vulnerability she'd seen when he talked about his childhood, she saw past his handsome face to the man inside. She was left feeling a bit like those thoughtless teens back in school who'd judged Jean Anne by her face. She'd judged Niccolò by his looks and tabloid stories, which, she now knew from personal experience, could have been a pack of lies.

At the end of the meal, Sam saw that Niccolò was tiring, so she offered to get the car and take him home. Niccolò vehemently refused, saying there was nothing wrong with his legs. They weren't finished with the real business of their trip into town, according to Nic. He still meant to put an end to speculation about them, even though she said she didn't care what anyone thought of her. And she really didn't. The family's reputation was Abby's hang-up. Not hers.

Still, Niccolò insisted they go to the drugstore in town, where he made fun of the article while in line. He did the same at the grocery store, where he insisted she get her groceries to give them the excuse to be there. She argued that, by returning there, she was reneging on her threat to Ron to never shop there again, but he said it was worth the opportunity.

They stopped in several shops on the way to the car. In one, he bought a T-shirt for Jamie. In a boutique, he asked her for help with sizes for her sisters, but, all on his own, he picked out the perfect style of a blouse for Caro and a flowing skirt perfect for Abby. All the while, Niccolò made sure everyone knew they were gifts for his godmother's daughters to thank them for taking him in and helping him heal.

She'd been a bit hurt that he hadn't tried to pick out something at her sisters' favorite boutique for her but, after they'd passed the ag store, Sam realized Niccolò had disappeared. When she turned to make a comment to him and he was no longer with her, she retraced her steps, looking in two stores before spotting him inside the ag. He stood in line holding the most unromantic a gift a man could buy a woman. And she was so touched, she told him she'd pick him up there and fled before he saw the tears filling her eyes. How could he know a top-of-the-line pair of work gloves were not just what she needed but what she'd want, too?

On the way home she asked why he'd decided on them, thinking he'd tell her they were as far as possible from a gift a lover would buy his current amour. Instead, he mentioned a top-of-the-line, professional potholder he'd noticed Abby using in Cliff Walk Bed-and-Breakfast's kitchen. After a pause, he went on to say Sam had lovely hands that were no less important than her sister's.

Sam was still stuck on the "lovely hands" remark. Even later, in the privacy of her room, she gazed down at her callused hands, perplexed by his comment. Her hands simply were not lovely. They were deeply tan in spite of all the sunscreen she slathered on each day. She had short and blunt nails—easier to get the dirt out from under them. She rarely polished them—it would only chip. Like his comment about Jean Anne, the one about her hands had been said in such a matter-of-fact way it rang true.

"Maybe he hit his head in the accident, too," she muttered, turned out the light and slid down in her bed, determined to get to sleep. She didn't have time to sit up, staring at her hands and wondering about the inner workings of Niccolò Verdini's mind. Five o'clock in the morning would come at the same time of the day, whether she had eight minutes' or eight hours' sleep.

Two mornings later, the sound of thunder startled Sam awake. "No! No! No!" she shouted, and bounded out of bed. She ran to the window and stared out at the tumbling river though a curtain of heavy rain. The end of a one day reprieve from rotten weather. "How can it be a thunderstorm? It was sixty-five yesterday! It's July, for God's sake! How much colder can it get?"

"Samantha, are you all right?" Niccolò called through her door as he knocked.

Sam threw open the door a moment later. "How can it be raining again?" she demanded.

Niccolò sighed. "All that shouting was about the weather?" He took a deep breath. "After you went to bed, the temperature started to climb. The weather person on the eleven o'clock news said a new front would move down from Canada and the clash of the low and high pressure was sure to spark thunderstorms. Your mother saw no sense in waking you with bad news when there was nothing you could do about it. She came in and turned off your alarm since you can hardly work in the fields in this," he explained, sweeping a hand toward the downpour outside her window.

Heedless of her dress—or lack of it—she fell back on the bed and closed her eyes. "Go away and leave me to my misery, then."

Niccolò didn't leave. He didn't move. She grew conscious of his silent presence and opened her eyes again.

His were watchful and something else that made her realize she wore only an oversized sleep shirt and panties. Self-conscious suddenly, Sam sat up. "What?" she snapped, not even knowing what it was she questioned.

He blinked as if startled out of a trance. "Mrs. Canton. She asks if I would check with you to see if you want her to fix you something for breakfast."

Sam huffed out a breath. No sense taking her bad mood out on him. "Sure. Tell her a omelet'll do. I'll be down in a few minutes."

Niccolò nodded, still wearing that same odd expression. There was an intensity in his eyes that had turned them black as coal. Then he just turned on his heel and left. She watched him stride down the hall; his lean body had a fluid grace that reminded her of a cat on the prowl.

The man was a walking, talking advertisement for sex. Hot sex. Passionate sex. Any-way-you-want-it sex. No wonder women worldwide threw themselves at him. All he had to do was fix those dark, sexy, intense eyes on her and she found herself wondering about things she'd given almost no thought to for years.

Sam shook her head, dislodging that thought. Other women—not her. She and Niccolò were only ever going to be friends. Friends. Pals. All she had to do was think of his usual women to know how it had to be. She was not a statuesque showgirl. She was certainly not a beauty queen or a model. Nor did she have the sophistication of the princess he'd been seen squiring around sometime last year. It was no surprise that, no matter how attractive she found him, he only wanted to be her friend.

Sam found Niccolò sitting at the big, round table when she entered the breakfast room. In front of him was a box of one of the most ridiculous breakfast cereals on the market. "Choco-Squares? If Jamie sees them, Caro's going to find herself in the middle of a food war." She picked up the offending box. "He isn't allowed anything that has sugar in the first four ingredients. Let's see. Wheat. Sugar. Oh, now, this is a real healthy way to start a day."

Niccolò shook his head, shamefaced. "Before I came to your evil country, I had never heard of Choco-Squares. Now, I fear, I have become addicted." He was teasing her! He had to be. She set the box down as he continued, "I promise there is no worry for Jamie. I keep them locked in my room."

She saw his lips twitch. "You're such a nut. You really had me going," she said and, laughing, went to pick the box up to toss it out.

Niccolò grabbed it as if she were taking away his next fix. "Hey. Where do you go with my breakfast?"

Sam crossed her arms and eyed him. "Are you going to tell me you actually eat that stuff?"

"Here's your omelet, Nic," Hannah Canton, their housekeeper, said as she walked into the room and slid a plate with a perfect veggie omelet in front of Niccolò.

Sam narrowed her eyes. "Choco-Squares, huh?"

Niccolò burst out laughing. It was such a lighthearted

sound Sam had to smile. "There. That is much better. Laughter is good medicine, no?"

Dropping down into a chair, she stared at him. "I repeat my verdict from the other day. You're a nut!"

"He may be a nut, young lady," Hannah said, "but it's been too long since you've even cracked a smile at this table. I've been worrying that my cooking's off."

"Not you, Mrs. Canton, but her grapes," Niccolò explained.

Hannah sighed and propped her hands on her more-than-ample hips. "It's Hannah, not Mrs. Canton. If you'd known my mother-in-law, you'd understand the difference. It's either *Hannah* or I go back to calling you *Niccolò*."

He dipped his head a bit. "Perish the thought! *Hannah,* thank you for the lovely breakfast."

"That's better, young man. And as for you, your omelet is all ready." She shook her head and clicked her tongue. "Hard as you work, you just don't eat enough."

Sometimes it felt as if she'd lived her life in a constant battle with weight. But she'd finally come to a place where she realized that she had a short, compact body. She was never going to be tall and willowy like her mother and sisters. She just wasn't built that way and being unhealthy wasn't going to change a thing for the better. She was well muscled because of her work, and she no longer thought about her figure one way or another. If her appetite had been off of late, it was due to intestinal distress because of the problems with her health and worry over her vines.

"I eat plenty," she told Hannah. "I just haven't had much of an appetite. Bring on the omelet. Okay?"

Minutes later, Hannah returned with a second perfect omelet. Niccolò broke the silence after the housekeeper left. "Samantha, I have been thinking about your water problem. I noticed you continue to cultivate the base of the plants."

Sam dropped her fork, appetite gone. She put her elbow on the table, leaned her chin on the palm of her hand and said sarcastically, "Gosh! Thanks for reminding me. I'd forgotten for two whole minutes. I've been trying to get the poor things some air. I even hauled away some of the soil and dumped dry soil around the plants." She shook her head. "Then it rained, packed it all down again and ruined a week of backbreaking work."

"Do you mind a suggestion? I don't want to stand on your feet but—"

Samantha dropped her head onto her arm, shaking with laughter. She heard Niccolò sigh. "What did I say? I am rarely so amusing to my team members."

She sat up and wiped her tearing eyes. "I'm sorry, Niccolò. Everything in my life is a mess and, I guess, you're just like a pressure valve sometimes. I'm really not trying to make fun of you. And the members of your team probably don't say anything when you mess up an idiom because you're a god to them." She gestured with her hand as if picturing a marquee and his name in lights. "The Italian Dynamo."

"I don't know whether I should be insulted or flattered. Suppose I opt for just asking what I said that so amused you?"

"It's *tread* or *step on my toes,* not *stand on my feet.*"

Niccolò's forehead wrinkled in confusion. "There is a difference?"

"I'm afraid it's just another fine line you have to walk. So what's your suggestion about the vines. Will's leaving really left me up a creek. That means—"

Nic held up his hand. "This one I know. He left when you needed his expertise. You've never dealt with a wet season like this, have you?"

Sam shook her head. "We have such good drainage it was never an issue before. I've pulled out all my old textbooks. I even called the school to ask one of my old professors but they're still on break."

"It is quite simple. Stop cultivating the plants. No more disturbing the soil. The dirt will have hardened with the heavy downpour all through the night. After it dries on top it will form a—" he thought for a moment to get the right word "—crust. The rain will run off the hard shell. In drought, you keep the soil cultivated to the depth of—" He tried to show her the depth between his hands, but his right hand was still nearly useless to him. Frustrated he went on. "An easy way to remember it is the depth of a new pencil. Your soil would then pull in up to two inches of rain or irrigation with no runoff."

Rather than be relieved, Sam was instantly ashamed. Had she asked Niccolò when her mother suggested it, she'd have saved herself and several vineyard workers a lot of backbreaking work. She gazed at him through blurred vision, and only realized tears had filled her eyes when they overflowed and streaked down her cheeks. Trying to hide them, she looked away, but by then Niccolò was sliding into the chair next to her, wrapping his good arm around her trying to offer comfort.

How was she supposed to stay just friends with him when he did sweet things like pat her back and tell her not to worry so much?

## *Chapter Six*

Nic was in a near panic. He had come to know Samantha well enough to be sure she didn't cry easily. He'd even go so far as to say she probably never cried at all. So what had just happened? What had he said? He'd only been trying to help. Surely, she knew she hadn't actually killed the vines.

"*Cara,* it's okay. You've done them no permanent damage. Vines live for decades. They are quite hardy. It takes more than one overly rainy season to destroy them. Much more."

"I know that." She sniffled. "It's just that I was so stubborn about you. When Will left, Mama said you might be able to help me if I needed advice, but I refused to ask you. I worked so hard. If I'd asked you, I wouldn't have spent the money on the topsoil. Or on the day laborers I'd hired. And all because I judged you unfairly. I'm sorry, Niccolò."

Nic took his arm from around Samantha and sat back. He wanted to look into her expressive eyes. To gauge her feelings if at all possible. Hers was a face that would be at home in a commercial for fresh-scrubbed skin or outdoor sports. There was a golden glow about her most days, though today she looked a bit pale. The more he got to know her, the more he knew he could trust her more than he'd ever trusted another woman other than his *nonna* and his *padrina*. As a friend, he reminded himself. She was to be only a friend.

"I am no fool, Samantha. I know why you didn't trust me. Apologies are unnecessary. You had no way of knowing how tabloids operate. I imagine you judged me to be like your father. You didn't trust me. Now I hope you do. If I am to be honest, I must admit I gave the tabloids room to speculate about me. They felt free to blow each of my relationships out of proportion because I gravitate toward a certain kind of woman."

"Why do you?"

He grimaced and then grinned, refusing to be ashamed because he was a healthy man. "Because I am no monk. Nor a saint. Nor do I wish to be. I enjoy making love to beautiful women. None of them have ever wanted more of me than physical pleasure, which is all I wanted from them. None of them could ever touch my heart and so could never hurt me as my mother had."

She stared at him, then rolled her eyes. "But that's because they're all such shallow bimbos."

Nic laughed. "There you go again, being tactful, holding back your opinions," he teased, and then sighed. "Perhaps, you are right. So tell me what else has you so low. It is more than the grapes and the adverse weather. I don't think you would be this upset over grapes and rain."

"The farming was supposed to be my part of the business. My whole family's counting on me. Caroline, Abby and Mama have all done their part. We have mortgage payments to make. And there's no grace period. The banker who helped Mama arranged the loan has worked behind the scenes to almost guarantee we'll fail. He's also the mayor of Hopetown. He blocked the permits on Bella Villa for so long that it wasn't up and running in time to hit the earnings projected for it. Because of that, we nearly missed our payment last summer. You actually met his mother in town earlier. Meryl Bryant."

"Ah, the busybody," he recalled just as he realized what was out of place. "Why is there no talk of your difficulties with the grapes at the evening meal when everyone is together?"

"I know they know, but I don't want to burden them further with a blow-by-blow account of the crop failure. I just can't."

"Your mother and sisters aren't foolish women. Or foolish in business. They do know about the trouble you face. They would never blame you for the weather or the problems caused because of it."

"It's my job to find a way around what nature throws at me."

"But nothing in nature is flawless. You strive for perfection where there can be none. As a farmer, you must bend and change as the weather does. This year, all you can do is your best. It's all any farmer can do."

"Don't you understand? I *have* to make this work. I'm the disappointing daughter. The slob. The one who dresses like—" she looked down at herself "—like this. I'm the daughter my father called—"

He held up his hand stopping her from repeating James Hopewell's nastiness. "Your father is gone, *cara,*" he reminded her instead. Thinking of how her father had treated her made his heart ache for the impressionable child and adolescent she'd been. He couldn't help but remember thinking Zia had made a silk purse of a sow's ear when he'd noticed how lovely Samantha looked at Caro's wedding. He was as ashamed of his reactions that day as she'd said she was over hers toward him. To tell her of his own shortsighted thoughts would be anything but kind, however.

She huffed out a deep breath. "Just because he died doesn't mean the things he'd said and done don't affect me."

"But he can hurt you no longer if you refuse to give him that power over you. He can belittle you no longer. As for how you dress, your career is a physical one and it would be quite ridiculous to dress for a garden party while working in the fields. And, no, you are not as tall and willowy as your sisters are. But you are still lovely.

Your face is the face of an angel. And here is a secret, *cara:* Some men like a woman with natural curves."

Samantha smiled, gratitude making the wedges of green in her eyes shine a bit brighter. How had he missed her beauty for even a moment? It was a good thing she had no interest in him because if she did, he didn't know if he could resist his building attraction to her.

"You're a very sweet man, Niccolò Verdini."

He had to grin at that. "No one has ever called me sweet."

It looked as if she were going to add something, but the phone rang and Hannah called out that the call was for her.

Deep in thought, Nic went back to his seat and finished his breakfast. Perhaps, given time, Samantha would tell him what it was she'd left out. He knew there was something else. Something important and, if he wasn't wrong, it was something she had not shared with her family. He didn't see how in so loving a family she could keep so deep a secret, but it seemed she did just that. She worked so hard at hiding her fear of failure and this other, more personal pain that he knew it had to be exhausting.

By the end of that first full week of July, they'd had a string of three perfect Pennsylvania summer days. It was eighty-five degrees by two in the afternoon with low humidity. Nic decided to walk to the winery and stroll through the rows of vines. He didn't often venture there because the place made him homesick, and going home wasn't an option for him.

Once he'd climbed the long, steep stone driveway and rounded the last bend, Nic realized the winery complex, Cliff Walk Bed-and-Breakfast and Bella Villa no longer made him homesick. He was quite startled when the truth hit him. This place, this family, had come to mean home to him.

The air was clean and a warm wind blew across the plateau. The river far below looked like a sparkling, blue ribbon wending its way along the valley that separated Pennsylvania and New Jersey with exquisite beauty.

He turned from the cliffs and strolled among the vines, then, breathed in the calm atmosphere. The vines showed a bit of damage due to the excess water, but he was sure it wasn't too late to rescue the season. There was a marked absence of workers today, telling him Samantha had taken his advice. He crouched down and noted that a crust had already formed at the base of the vines. Left undisturbed, it would shed water rather well.

As he got back to his feet, the wind carried the sound of someone in pain. Nic stood still, listening, trying to decide where it had come from. He pivoted and cocked his head to hone in on the sound. His gaze met an equipment shed. The door was wedged open with a rake but there was no one around. Then he heard the noise again and took off, jogging uphill.

Inside, he found Samantha. She was crouched in a corner, with her back against the wall and her forehead on her knees. Her arms were wrapped around her legs and her hands clutching each other in a white-knuckled grip. If her tears had not broken his heart, watching her trying to smother the sounds of her pain about ripped the worthless thing right out of his chest.

"Samantha. Samantha. What is it, *cara?*"

Her horrified gaze met his and he knew what it was she hadn't told him earlier in the week. Not exactly what was wrong, but he knew that whatever had her nearly writhing in the corner of an equipment shed was a large part of it. He wanted to scoop her up and take her to where she would get help. But, of course, he couldn't. His arm and shoulder made him all but worthless as a rescuer since he couldn't carry her very far at all. Instead, he slid down the wall next to her and just sat, waiting for her to tell him what she needed of him.

Samantha, though, went back to her previous position, hiding her face and ignoring him.

"Is there anything I can do?" he asked finally.

"You could go away and pretend you didn't find me like this."

He could tell the order came from between clenched teeth. What he didn't know was whether they were clenched in anger or pain. With Samantha, it was most probably both. "No, Samantha," he told her. "I would not leave a dog to suffer like this alone. Are we not trying to be friends? I thought friends care for each other. I would be a poor friend to leave you like this. No?"

"It's personal, okay? And it's nothing I'm going to talk to you about."

"I can be a very good listener. It is clear this is something else you try to keep your family from worrying over. Am I correct?"

"Anyone ever compare you to a pit bull?"

"One of those dogs that latches on to something and will not let go?" He chuckled. "No. I think this is the first time, but then, this is the first time I cared enough to be a pit bull. Samantha, it is clear you are ill. If you will not tell me, I can go over to the winery and bring Zia Juliana back with me."

Samantha wiped her teary eyes on her sleeve and looked up at him. "I've tried so hard to deal with this, but there's no answer. It's like my body's betraying me."

"Perhaps if you told me what this is?"

"I told you. It's personal," she snapped.

"Pain usually is. I don't believe yours is all physical. I think your heart is in pain, as well."

"Take a hint, will you?" she told him. "It's female stuff, okay?"

"Do you think I am someone who will not understand, or are you just embarrassed? While I am not quite the Lothario the tabloids say I am, I have lived with my share of women and their personal matters."

She sighed in what seemed to be defeat. "I have something wrong. Inside. It's called endometriosis. And now I'm out of options. I was on a drug therapy for a year that worked but a year was the longest I could stay on it. When I went off the medication, it came back with a vengeance. My mother and sisters know about it because the problems have been around since I was fourteen, but they don't know the drug ultimately failed. And they don't know what it means for me."

"And what does it mean? This kind of pain each month?"

She shook her head, her tears returning. "That isn't the cause of the pain today. It's affected all my organs now. I'm in pain most of the time now. My only option is a hysterectomy."

Now he understood those times when she'd looked pale. And it had been pain that had dulled her usually sparkling hazel eyes. It was so sad to think of her continuing on with her hardworking days while fighting pain as well as adversity.

Sadder still, was thinking of her never having a child. She was so wonderful with her nephew and would be the kind of caring, nurturing mother every child deserved. Her heart truly must be breaking. There should be some way to fix this. "Is there nothing else to be done? Perhaps in Europe where medical procedures are not so stringently overseen by the government…"

"I could have a baby now, but conceiving might even be a problem." She shook her head. "Even if I didn't feel creepy about picking my baby's father from a looseleaf binder full of personal profiles at a fertility clinic, my medical insurance doesn't cover that option."

He didn't even need to ask about the more natural method. He'd been there long enough to known there were no men in her life. "I see you with Jamie. You would be such a wonderful mother," he commented instead. "Life is so often not fair."

"Yeah," she agreed, and chuckled, but it was a mirthless sound. Then she sniffled and once again hid her face by bowing her head toward her upraised knees. "Fair is just a weather forecast, but not even the weather has been fair lately, huh?" Her words, muffled by her position, had Nic straining to hear her.

He somehow resisted pulling her into his arms, simply agreeing with her in a voice that sounded choked in his own ears. He stopped himself from promising to make everything all right. There was only one way to do that, and he was smart enough to realize how insane the idea of fathering her child would be for him.

Fatherhood was something he knew he was unqualified for. Look at the only example he'd had—his own inadequate father. If ever there had been a woman whom he'd trust to rear his child, it was Samantha. But he knew he wasn't the man for her. She needed and deserved a man worthy of her sweetness. Her strong work ethic. Her honesty.

Remaining silent was the most difficult task he'd ever set for himself. Instead of trying to leap to the rescue and chance ruining her life, Nic stared out the open doors at row after row of slightly yellowed vines. He sighed. Life for Samantha seemed not to be fair in any way at all.

Later that night, Sam sat in her bed unable to sleep. She still couldn't believe she'd told Nic what she hadn't managed to find a way to tell her family. He was indeed becoming a friend.

A good friend.

That thought gave her pause. When he'd first arrived, Nic was clearly suffering from acute homesickness and not just the boredom he'd claimed. He'd even avoided the winery complex, which would have alleviated some of the restlessness caused by confinement at the manor. But he was at the winery all the time now. She often saw him strolling among the vines even on days when there were intermittent showers.

Today, while they walked back to her pickup, he'd all but begged her to call him Nic instead of Niccolò. He said he felt less foreign and more at home being addressed with the more American nickname given him by his team members. She thought the real meaning behind the request was that he was searching for something—a place to call home.

Was Hopetown becoming that place?

He did seem less restless, his smile more genuine. And he was comfortable enough after their heart-to-heart on the trip into town to let her and everyone else in the family see behind the veneer of the casual, sexy playboy all the way to the kind, genuinely nice man he kept hidden in an effort to protect his heart. She felt good about that.

At least she hadn't failed him as a friend as she had failed at everything else in her life. Not only was she failing at farming, but she was still a failure at everything to do with being a woman. Even reproduction.

Nic thought she was foolish to feel like a failure but she did. She just did. It was easy for him to give her advice such as ignoring the things her father had said to and about her. Just look at Nic. He was an Adonis, the embodiment of tall, dark and handsome. And he was a success at his career, even if his profession was dangerous and had caused a huge rift in his family. He had the courage to walk through life on his terms.

And he could father children worldwide if he wanted to! Of that, she had no doubt.

Sam stilled at the thought. Nic could father a child… her child.

*No.*

There were too many family connections. It was an insane idea. She'd lost her mind. Nic just seemed to have had that effect on her from the moment she'd met him.

But, oh, just the thought of his hands—his mouth— on her. Him becoming part of her in so intimate an act. Sam suddenly felt hot and achy in places she'd rarely thought of before Nic came along. Sleeping with him for the sole purpose of conceiving wouldn't be the chore she'd thought it would be. Instead, it would be a memorable experience. The most memorable of her life, she'd bet. She had the idea that Nic was good at everything he put his hands to. It would be a sort of three-for-one deal—pleasure, a baby and the bonus of a possible five-year remission of her condition.

The trouble was, Sam wasn't sure it would or could be for the sole purpose of a child. Or the dual purpose of conceiving a baby and experiencing the pleasure she knew Nic would provide. Because she liked Nic. Cared about him. Even trusted him. It would mean too much. Her heart would be involved. It couldn't help but be.

And there was her mother and his *nonna*. Both women would have a fit if she became a single parent by conventional means with Nic as the father and neither of them would understand his not offering marriage.

Marriage? To Nic? She shook her head. *Get real, Sammy. Marriage isn't even part of Nic's vocabulary. Nor is fatherhood.* She punched her pillow, rolled over and closed her tired eyes. Unfortunately, after all the thinking about Nic, sleep brought with it dreams of him. His sensual mouth kissing hers. His full lips following his hands as they played over the intimate places on her body.

Consequently, she woke ready and willing. And alone.

## Chapter Seven

Nic couldn't sleep. Especially now that the sun was up. Maddeningly, sleep had evaded him all night long. He pushed himself into a sitting position and admitted he'd been looking for an excuse to abandon his futile attempts to nod off. His thoughts still in a whirl, he got out of the comfortable bed that had morphed into a torture rack. A long walk to clear his head would serve him better than more tossing and turning. It had nearly worked yesterday, but then he'd found Samantha.

Samantha, her predicament and her pain-filled eyes, haunted him even now that the sun was brightening the day. He was doubly impressed by her after learning her crushing secret. Deeply saddened by her hidden pain, she was also strong and brave, continuing to carry on in secret, day after day.

He wanted to help.

Exactly how he wasn't sure. Or even if he should try. Since when did he allow himself to become embroiled in difficulties in the lives of others? Never. But then no one he knew had wanted to be involved with him when he'd been injured. No one except his teammates had come to see him in the hospital. And then the circuit had moved on—and, of course, they'd had to, as well. His flowers had wilted. His fruit basket had been empty but for a few hard candies. He'd been so alone. Then Zia Juliana had swooped in and demanded he return to Hopewell Manor. And she and her daughters had taken him into their home. Into their family.

That was why he should help Samantha. She was his friend. It was so new a concept to him, Nic wasn't even sure what it fully meant. All he knew was what he felt. Her problems were his, as well.

Intent on walking off his inner turmoil, Nic stepped out into the warm muggy dawn of a new day. A light fog hugged the ground and a profusion of tall trees obscured the horizon and therefore the kind of day it would be. Of course, he'd learned that in Pennsylvania there were many days when no one was sure what the weather held in store until it happened. A sunny day could turn stormy in a flash. Rain clouds could blow away and the sun could have the streets steaming in the blink of an eye.

He crossed the road at the foot of the manor's drive

and headed toward the vineyard. There was a newly cut nature path to the winery complex that began with a set of crude stone stairs that had been carved into the rocky hillside. The steps blended into the terrain so well he had missed them until Zia Juliana showed him where they began. She'd had them created after Jamie set off in a huff from the vineyard one day intent on climbing down the steep embankment to reach home.

After gaining the top of the plateau that held the family's enterprises, Nic almost immediately came upon the new home of Caroline and Trey Westerly. He stopped to admire the French château design that was evident now that the house was nearly complete. Soon, it would be ready for the newest branch of the Hopewell family.

Workmen were trying to solve problems with the heating-and-cooling system and the kitchen countertops were being installed. Nic spoke briefly with a plumber who was off to another job but was due back that afternoon to finish his work once the counters were finished. After that, the Westerly family would move from the manor house.

The acreage on the plateau Zia Juliana had purchased after her divorce was larger than Nic had thought because much of it remained heavily forested and undeveloped. The best part was that, after carving out the acreage for the vineyards, the business complex and the parklike setting surrounding Cliff Walk, there was still surplus land. Zia Juliana had deeded over three separate two-acre plots to each of her daughters for homes.

Each plot sat on far-flung corners of the plateau and

overlooked different views of the rolling hills or of the river valley below. Still, there was a great deal of land left over so Samantha had set up a woodland preserve of a sort. She'd cut nature trails that wound across the plateau and provided the customers of Cliff Walk with access to all of the spectacular views the Hopewell property had to offer.

After bidding goodbye to the workmen, Nic walked on from Caro and Trey's house, soon reaching a place where the property fell away to reveal the valley and river below. It was quite a view of the Hopewell Manor property and the twisting river tumbling by behind it. Looking down at the manor, one word came to mind. *Family.*

He envied them their strong sense of family. It was perhaps one of the pieces missing in his fractured life. Now, as he turned away from the river to follow the cracked-stone drive leading from the Westerly house, Nic's thoughts returned to those long moments under the water when he'd realized he would die leaving nothing of value behind. His new engine design might have added to his bank balance, but it would create a mere footnote in the history of the insular world of high-speed racing. As a legacy it was almost nonexistent.

That knowledge had left him feeling empty for weeks now.

It was an emptiness that bothered him a great deal and it had not lessened with time. Instead, the emptiness had grown. He remembered now that during some of those moments under the water, he'd thought of his sister but not of his hatred for her. He'd actually envied her the spoiled children of her unholy alliance with Carlo Bianco. It hadn't made sense then. How could Nic wish he'd had children when he'd sworn over and over that he would never father a child? His reason had certainly not changed. What kind of example of fatherhood did he have to model himself after? His father? He would **die be**fore scarring a child as his father had scarred him and Gina.

Nic noticed a fallen tree off to the side of the cracked-stone pathway so he decided to sit awhile and collect his thoughts further. After hearing Samantha talk about her loss, he understood better why Gina and her demon seeds had come into his thoughts at that critical time when his life seemed to be at an end. Children were a legacy. A continuation. A form of im-mortality. He had always thought that sort of sentiment didn't matter to him.

Now he faced the truth.

It did.

It mattered very much. He understood Samantha's urge to have a child better than most people who knew him might think he would. Nic sank to the fallen trunk in near shock at where his deliberations had taken him. He was actually tempted to offer to father Samantha's child.

Had he lost his mind?

Staggered though he was by the very idea, Nic felt compelled to examine it thoroughly. Perhaps it would not be so insane an idea if he handled it properly. He would first have to assure Samantha that he would immediately step aside and not interfere in any way with her raising of the child. That way, they would both have what they wanted. She would have her child and know the father but not have to be dishonest to the man about the pregnancy in order to ensure that she could raise her child without the risk of interference. And he would have his continuation—his immortality—without fearing the damage he might cause by being a full-time, active father.

Samantha would be fine raising a child on her own. She had her family for support. Look at the way they had all pitched in to help Caroline raise the orphaned half brother she'd adopted. Jamie was a sweet but difficult child because of his special problems. With the aid of aunts and a grandmother, however, he'd progressed so far that his disability was nearly unnoticeable.

Nic sighed. Perhaps it was not a bad idea, but it would never work. Nonna would never forgive him if he helped bring a child into the world and failed to give it his name, especially with Samantha involved. Besides that, his grandmother was of a different generation and would be immensely ashamed and hurt by it. Nic would not wound her for even this important a personal reason. Since there was little chance that Nonna and Zia Juliana would fail to learn he'd had an affair with Samantha, he could do nothing to help her.

Nic sighed in disgust then stopped; his mind, his heart stilled. An affair sounded so tawdry with Samantha involved. He knew he could never have done it. He didn't want to just leave a child behind like excess baggage, either. He was disgusted at the idea of being yet another anonymous sperm-donor father. There were enough of those in the world.

Though he knew he couldn't chance having day in, day out contact with a child for the sake of the child, for the sake of that same child Nic would want to offer financial support. He would also want to add an emotional grounding of at least being a long-distance part of his or her life. If he acknowledged birthdays, attended milestone celebrations and perhaps had his child for some holidays, he'd be around enough to make sure his child felt valued by him. Something he had felt from his own father. Unfortunately his father had also made him feel owned and not loved. If Nic kept his contact light, it would lessen the danger that he would make a parental mistake.

And it would mean remaining part of Samantha's life. He could only see that as an advantage. Their child would see that its parents valued each other. Nic would remain Samantha's friend, plus, he would have some small carefully thought-out input into the future of their child.

Restless, Nic stood and started on his way to the vineyard along one of Samantha's nature trails. Even with his attention diverted to picking his way along, he couldn't banish the idea now that he'd examined it so closely. He guessed the question really was, was there any way to make what he'd been toying with happen? Had he created a perfect dream where none could exist?

If it were just him, Samantha and their child involved, Nic thought it, indeed, would be a possibility.

He and Samantha would be loving friends—each getting something important out of a child born from their short relationship.

But again, Nonna would never understand. And Zia Juliana, though she would perhaps understand that he'd only been trying to help, would be upset if the tabloids got hold of the story of Samantha's pregnancy. He frowned. He was often the darling of the press. Most of the time they put the reason for the breakups on the woman. If they cast Samantha as the villain of the piece, it would eventually have an impact on their child, as well as Samantha.

Remembering the reactions of the townspeople to the false story about them, he was afraid Samantha would quickly come to regret her decision to give birth out of wedlock.

Nic stopped in his tracks. Wedlock? Marriage? How had he arrived there? Shocked though he was by the idle thought, he could not banish the idea, either. Marriage was something he'd only contemplated once and that was a way to circumvent Nonno's will.

But wait! He'd rejected the idea because he knew he could never trust any of the women of his acquaintance. He trusted Samantha. She was the most honorable woman he'd ever met—except Zia Juliana and Nonna.

A short marriage to Samantha would do more than lend legitimacy to their baby. It would scuttle Gina's hopes for getting more money from the estate Nonno had left them.

He thought for a moment, not wanting to rush into

offering a solution to Samantha until he'd looked at all possibilities. It was true that Nonna would be upset over a divorce, but not nearly as upset as she would be over a great-grandchild born out of wedlock. For a full year, she would be happy to know he was settled. A dream come true for her. She need never know it was a bargain and not a real marriage.

The important thing was that it would give both him and Samantha what they wanted most. After looking at it every way he could, nothing came to mind that would deter him.

It could be perfect!

It would be good for both of them. He would make sure the second half of his grandfather's bequest to him stayed out of the grasping hands of his sister. He would have a child to carry on his name and memory when he was gone. Samantha would get to be a mother, which she richly deserved. And she'd avoid the scorn of her small community and of the world at large when the tabloids learned of her relationship with him.

Nic broke through the trees uphill from Bella Villa and noticed Samantha, Caroline and Abby having their weekly meeting on the roof terrace. The morning sun caught in Samantha's hair and it shimmered even at this great distance. He longed to run his fingers through its spun gold and perhaps he would, but there was more to think of and consider first.

There were some foreseeable problems. In order to meet his grandfather's stipulation, they would have to remain married for more than a year. They would have to pretend to love each other for that long in order to keep their bargain a secret. But since they both did care for one another, there should be no difficulty there. They'd become friends. He would never trust any other woman to adhere to a bargain like this, but he trusted Samantha implicitly.

The second problem was also related to the one-year stipulation. His presence in Samantha's life for that long would inevitably spark tabloid stories for even longer. They would be divorcing, after all, and there was little chance that reporters wouldn't invade her privacy often. Nic realized then that he needed to offer something else to counterbalance that kind of annoyance.

And he knew exactly what to offer. It was something she would have difficulty turning down because her whole family would benefit. He'd managed to get Zia Juliana to tell him how much they still owed on their loan. The amount was fully half of the bequest he was trying to keep from Gina's grasping hands but without Samantha's help, his sister would have it all.

Just imagining Gina's anger when she heard of his marriage made Nic chuckle. He would pay off the Hopewells' loan, freeing Sam and her family from worry over the deceitful banker who appeared to be after their business and their land.

Nic knew he would have no problem spending the extra time with Samantha to see that she conceived. He thought she was one of the most admirable people he'd ever met. He grinned. The procreation part of the bargain would be no sacrifice on his part. He grew more attracted to her every day. Even thinking about the possibility of being intimate with her aroused him.

The real question was, how did Samantha feel about him?

A few times, he'd thought he'd seen attraction gleaming in her incredible hazel eyes but he couldn't be sure. Samantha was rather an enigma as far as he was concerned. He should always know what she was thinking or feeling because her emotions showed on her face. But Nic was often unsure of what he was seeing in her expression. That was most likely because he'd never met a woman like her.

Around Samantha he was often left feeling as inexperienced with women as she was with men. It was a bit maddening but also rather refreshing. It made everything he experienced around her—with her—feel new and different. Perhaps, that alone accounted for his attraction to her. Perhaps, she was exactly the person he needed at this crossroad in his life that the accident had placed him at.

Right then, all Nic was sure of was that he wanted her. Wanted to feel her in his arms. Wanted to give her the child she ached for. Wanted to feel her every reaction to the things he would teach her about herself as a woman and about him as a man.

Now all that remained was for him to propose this bargain of a marriage and see if she thought he'd lost his mind or if she was as desperate for a child as he was. He shrugged. Why put it off? He'd go to Bella Villa and ask her, he decided, and surged forward, startling a blue jay who had, no doubt, been searching the ground for its breakfast. It, in turn, startled him.

Nic laughed at the bird who scolded him from the branch of a tree high overhead. "Good morning, *signora*," he called to the angry jay and realized he felt buoyant and completely happy for the first time since the accident.

Nic started off toward Bella Villa, again aching with a need like he'd never known. Yes, everything was new because of Samantha and the things they could give each other. Now all he had to do was wait for her meeting to be over.

"As long as neither of you have anything to add, I guess that's it," Caro said, as she squared and stacked her papers on the mosaic tabletop, ending their once-a-week breakfast meeting.

Abby shook her head and started stacking their soiled plates. "I wanted to mention that the produce from our new source is picture-perfect."

"What about the butcher?" Sam asked anxiously.

"The butcher you recommended only handles prime meats. The guests this week have been raving about the sausage and the dinners, too."

That got Caro's attention off her stacking. "So, do you think you'll go ahead with the idea of opening the dining room for guests who want to eat the evening meal at Cliff Walk?"

"Well, I was going to wait till next week to give you the word, but they really like being able to eat dinner here. Genevieve is one happy chef to have full-time work and she loves the meats. She says the steaks practically tenderize themselves. Thanks for pushing us to change suppliers, Sammy."

Sam shrugged and smiled sheepishly. "I had a purely selfish motive and you know it," she reminded Abby ruefully, shaking her head. "Ron Johnson just really got to me this time. I was threatening to take our business elsewhere before I thought it out completely. I should be thanking you two for going along with it and not making me eat crow."

"Well, if I'd have known he had the gall to talk to you the way he apparently has in the past, he'd have lost our business long ago," Caro told her, green eyes flashing with indignation. "And he still might lose more. If I field any calls from his headquarters, you'd better believe I'll be letting them know why we aren't using them anymore."

"Ditto," Abby sang out.

It warmed Sam's heart that her sisters cared so much and had stuck by her, even though switching to three new suppliers instead of using just one had caused them both extra work. Maybe Nic was right. Maybe she should tell them what was up with her health instead of carrying the burden alone.

Just as Sam was about to bring up her problem, she heard the scrape of footsteps moving upward on the outside stairs to the roof terrace. She looked across the scattered mosaic dining sets to see Nic gain the top step and turn toward them. His eyes met hers and held.

"Okay then," Abby said as she noticed Nic. She stood quickly, placing their already stacked breakfast dishes in the picnic basket she'd brought them in. "I have breakfast to help get on the table by nine o'clock for the guests. Have a good day, you two." She glanced at Nic again. "Hi, Nic. You're out and about early."

"I had some things on my mind so I took a walk. I passed your new home. It is looking wonderful, Caro. You will move in soon?"

"The builder promised we'd have it any day. We'll see. He said that two months ago, but he can hardly be blamed for the weather that held up the stonework."

"No one can," Nic added, and Sam knew he'd said it for her benefit.

"Of course not," Caro added. "Well, if you'll excuse me, I have to drive Jamie to hippo therapy. He can't stand to be even a minute late for his horseback riding lesson. Have a nice day, guys. Hope you worked out whatever had you up so early, Nic," she added before leaving through the door to the inside of Bella Villa.

"And I really have to run, now," Abby said, and hurried off down the stairs Nic had just climbed.

"You look tired," Sam told him, and held up the carafe of coffee that had been her contribution to the meeting. "Sit down and have a cup. There's plenty left. Mama had a late night so she missed the meeting."

"Another date with her doctor friend?" Nic asked as he sank into the chair next to hers. "I thought she and Will would have patched up their differences by now."

Nic's nearness filled her with longing and made the

terrace garden feel closed in. She studiously avoided thinking about the things she felt when he was near. Instead, she forced her mind onto her mother and her date last night with Doctor David Kapp. "She's too busy trying to prove Will didn't mean anything to her to really look at how she feels about him. She'd accepted Will's apology when he'd called, but she won't let him come back. Which means he isn't really forgiven but politely frozen out."

"Your mother is too hot-blooded for that. She would…"

His voice faded as Sam began to shake her head. "No. Cool anger is something she learned from my father and his parents. She exploded when she found out who Will really was, but now she's calmed down. Until something breaks through her reserve, Will won't be welcomed back."

"And what of this Kapp?"

"It probably won't surprise you to hear this, but I don't trust him. And wonder of wonders, neither does Trey. My brother-in-law finally agrees with me about something."

"What kind of doctor is this Dr. Kapp?"

She grimaced. "Plastic surgeon to the rich and infamous."

"Being a plastic surgeon can be an honorable undertaking. When I was young, a friend was badly maimed in an accident. A doctor in Rome did wonders on his face and charged very little to his parents who were just poor farmworkers. Are you sure you are judging him fairly?"

She nodded. "Trey says Kapp works his magic on

rich, vain women with minor flaws. He never turns down a patient. He just operates and collects his fee. His card reads: 'Don't let them call you Grandma. Look younger than your daughter.' He's a snake oil salesman. Only, instead of selling false cures he's selling false youth. It's disgusting."

Nic's eyes narrowed in confusion. "Snake oil salesman?"

"They used to travel around the country selling fake cures."

Nick nodded. "We also have surgeons who fix what is already lovely in its uniqueness. It is a great problem that women are so critical of themselves. And that so many fear aging. But Zia Juliana would never have a surgery like that."

"I'm afraid he sees something other than a potential patient in Mama. I'm afraid when he looks at her, he really sees all this and assumes Mama is wealthier than she is."

"Then, perhaps, someone should mention to Dr. Kapp that all is not as it appears. Then we will see if he remains in her life."

"Unfortunately, he knows I don't like him so I'm not likely to get into a conversation where I can slip that in."

"I can. And I will, if you wish."

Sam felt her worry drain away. "That'd be great. One less thing to worry about. Thanks. I don't want to see her hurt, even though I don't think she has any real feelings for him. From where I sit, she's using him to forget Will. I'm just not sure she's even aware of it."

Nic had become a friend. A real friend. And her friend looked exhausted. "So, tell me, Niccolò Verdini, why do you look so tired and what had you up and about so early?"

"I could not stop thinking of your pain and sorrow. Finally at dawn, when I had not slept all night, I decided to see if a walk would help still my thoughts."

"Nic, don't. It isn't your problem. You're supposed to be regaining your strength—not sitting up all night thinking about my gloomy future. You're going to make me sorry I told you."

"Nonsense. I am all but recovered from my injuries. The cast comes off Friday. I am honored that you shared your problem with me."

"Did the walk help? Maybe you could get some sleep now if I drive you home."

Nic shook his head. "Yes and no. I could not stop thinking but the walk helped me think more efficiently. I believe I may have come up with an answer to at least part of your problem. Will you promise to trust me and listen to my idea before you react? It will sound like a—" he hesitated. "—like a crazy idea but I think it has great merit."

"I—I…sure." Sam frowned, uncertain, but determined not to hurt Nic by refusing to listen to his idea. "Sure, I'll listen. No harm ever came from just listening."

"I thought all night about the unfairness of your situation and I propose we make a bargain."

Sam frowned. "What kind of bargain?"

Nic stared at the mosaic tabletop, then looked back up at her. His dark eyes were wary—haunted. "In June it started with the accident."

What could his accident have to do with her illness? Or a bargain? She was about to ask but he started talking again.

"I was conscious under the water. I knew my life was ending."

She reached out and grabbed his hand. She had taunted him with how close death had been for him. And he'd known. He'd experienced what must have felt like death. "I didn't know. I was unforgivably cruel to you about it when you first came here. I'm always having to tell you I'm sorry."

Nic shook his head and waved off her apology. "You cared enough to warn me where I was headed. You could not have known I was already aware of how close death was or that my life has stood for nothing."

"I never said that! It just isn't so. You have friends. You invented that…that whatsit for the boat engines."

Once again, he sadly shook his head. "Have any of my so-called friends come here to see me? No. They have not. I will tell you why. Other than Jake and the rest of the team, I have only colleagues. Rivals. Ex-lovers. I have one true, very good friend. And she is in great need and pain just now. Last night I realized she is not the only one in need. I am, as well. Children are a legacy. A continuation. A form of immortality. Children carry on and remember us when we are gone. I thought to never have children. It is said we are the kind of parents our parents were."

"Well now, that's just plain stupid. You'd never try to tell your son how to live or cut him off for not agreeing and going his own way."

But Nic was shaking his head. "I have never been willing to risk emulating my father and therefore damaging the heart and soul of an innocent child."

"So that's another reason you only become involved with women who can't touch your heart and who you'd never want to have a future with."

"Yes. And so when Nonno Emidio died and his will demanded I marry by my thirtieth birthday and remain married for a year, I was angry but I resigned myself to forfeiting the second half of my share of his estate to my sister. I could trust none of the women of my acquaintance to marry for even a short time."

Sam didn't get it. "Nic, I'm sorry my situation brought up a lot of bad memories for you but why are you telling me all of this? Call me dense, but what does one have to do with the other?"

Nic raked a hand through his hair. "I am doing a poor job of this. I want to give you a child—my child. Because I trust you to raise our child."

Sam could only stare. She couldn't even pretend not to have thought of this. But she knew Dolores Verdini would go ballistic if Nic fathered an illegitimate child. She couldn't be responsible for Nic losing the one member of his family he still had. "No," she said unequivocally. "No way, Nic."

He blinked as if he'd never considered her refusal. "But why? I am not attractive to you? Being in my bed would be a chore?"

Sam laughed at his wounded pride, then she sobered. "Nic, you're practically a portrait of the gods. Don't be ridiculous. I'm concerned about Dolores."

He sighed. "I have thought of Nonna. I am proposing a temporary marriage, as well."

"Ma-marriage?"

"Marriage is the only way our families would not be hurt and angered by our actions. This would give me the rest of my inheritance and both of us a child to share. It need only last a year or a year and a half, at most. To make up for any notoriety our marriage brings you, I will pay off the bank loan on the winery immediately and we will have a friendly divorce when the terms of Nonno's will have been fulfilled."

"I would intrude very little into the child's life. After a few years, I would perhaps take him or her on a vacation now and again. To make sure the child does not feel underappreciated, I will always send birthday gifts. I will try to attend important events when I am asked."

Something was still off. "What do you get? So far, all you're talking about is solving my problems. Don't forget, I know how big that loan is."

"My sister will be thwarted in her quest to gain more of the estate of Nonno Emidio. Do not underestimate that as a bonus for me, and there will be money left over after the payment of the loan. Most important, I will have a child. I will know my child is happy with you as its mother. I will not leave this earth without leaving something behind to say I was here."

Sam stared at him. *He has no idea how lucky a child would be to have him as a father.* And it would be a waste of breath to try convincing him. That was when it hit her. What he was offering—proposing. He was offering her everything. He was trying to fix everything that was wrong with her life and asking so little in return it was pitiful. He was asking for her trust and offering his.

He had that and more. She had thought she wouldn't want her child's father in the picture. Now she couldn't imagine not having Nic be a part of both their lives. She knew in a flash of insight that she valued his friendship as she had nothing else in her life.

She didn't hesitate. She smiled and held out her hand. "You have yourself a bargain, Niccolò Verdini."

## Chapter Eight

Sam stood at the window of the MGM Grand's exclusive Skyloft that Nic had booked for them. The lights of Las Vegas and the stars above twinkled like diamonds in the inky night sky. The room had more than just a spectacular view, though. It came with a personal concierge, a butler and, most notably, a spalike bathroom that even had rose petals floating on the top of an infinity tub.

She didn't even want to think what this had cost. Used to traveling first-class all over the world, Nic had made all the arrangements. He'd booked the room, air flights, even the tastefully decorated wedding chapel, appointed in soft wood tones and shades of golden beige. The white and cream roses he had given her as a wedding bouquet had also been elegant in their simplicity. She looked down at the beautiful dress and shoes Nic had bought her. They'd come from Marshall Rousso's, a boutique he'd whisked her off to as they'd strolled along a path called Studio Walkway though the massive MGM Grand hotel.

It had all been a blur. A beautiful blur. And so easy. So effortless. So much easier than telling her mother. Which, to make it easy on Sam, Nic had done, as well. He'd gotten up at the end of dinner and moved to the chair next to her mother's and asked for her blessing. All he'd gotten had been a long moment of tense silence that Trey broke when he offered to break out a bottle of sparkling wine for a toast. Sam would be forever grateful to him for that. Juliana hadn't refused but had pulled Samantha aside as soon as she could...

"Are you sure you know what you're doing?" Juliana had asked as soon as Nic went off to begin looking into their travel arrangements. They'd planned to leave early Saturday since his cast was to come off Friday.

"I'm very sure, Mama," Sam'd promised.

Not convinced, Juliana'd countered, "But this is so sudden. You could barely tolerate Nic two weeks ago. Now the two of you are suddenly determined to run off and get married? You've never even gone on a date."

She'd known Juliana would be their toughest hurdle. Caro hadn't been able to say much. She and Trey had. agreed to marry to solve the complicated issue of Jamie's custody. Luckily, before their wedding, they'd realized each was marrying the other for love. Abby had been, as always, only concerned that no scandal surfaced involving the family name. As far as Abby was concerned, having her sister marry Nic was infinitely better than having her once again linked to him in a tabloid as his latest paramour.

"Our first date was a week ago," she'd told her mother. "We had a long lunch at the hotel. Then we went shopping for the gifts Nic wanted for all of you."

"And you. Nic bought you work gloves as I recall. That doesn't exactly spell romance."

Sam had grinned. "It does to me. He said my lovely hands deserved to be protected by the best." She'd held up her hands. They actually did look better already, but she was in no way ready for a new career as a hand model. "How much more romantic do you want?"

Juliana had blinked, clearly seeing her point. "But do you know each other well enough for such a big step?"

"The two of us have been living in the same house for five weeks. I found out how unfair and often untruthful the tabloids are when they turned a simple conversation in the vineyard into a tabloid affair. We've talked for hours at a time since then. Nic is so much more than the daredevil international playboy they make him out to be. I'd say we know each other really well. After all, neither of us has ever put on pretend good manners for the other."

Juliana'd smirked. "I know, dear. I've heard the fire-works between the two of you."

Sam'd huffed out a breath. "Okay. That's fair. We did fight. A lot. But only at first," she'd quickly added. "Don't you see? We cleared the air and we understand each other now. Many couples see each other less than

Nic and I have over a six-month-long courtship. And they mostly see each other on dates. Dates are all about phony manners and best behavior. Nic and I started out as enemies, got to be friends then figured out we want a deeper relationship. Would you rather he just take me to bed like he has all those others instead of caring enough to want to marry me?"

Her mother'd clearly had no rebuttal for that. "Then, get married here," Juliana'd countered. "We can put a lovely wedding together in weeks."

"We considered getting married here. That's what Nic assumed we'd do. But Mama, Nic only has one person to invite who really cares about him. I don't want him put in that position."

Juliana'd stared at her with such intensity, it had made Sam want to squirm. Then, to Sam's utter surprise, her mother'd slapped the table lightly and said, "It's settled, then. You'll go off to marry the love of your life and we'll have a small family party when you get back. That way, Nic will know he's part of our family now."

Relieved but feeling a little guilty that she'd misled her mother to think they were in love, Sam had thanked Juliana for her understanding and they'd hugged.

But she wasn't relieved now. She glanced toward the bedroom. There was a king-sized bed in there with padded suede headboards and footboards and it dammed well terrified her. Her mother had said she and Nic had never been on a date and Sam had countered with their lunch in town, but Juliana had been more correct than she'd remembered.

Sam had never been on a date. Period.

Sam had never been kissed, either.

Not by Nic. Not by anyone. She didn't really know how she'd managed to keep so impenetrable a barrier between her and the other half of the human race for so many years but she had. And now she was supposed to...

God! What had she been thinking?

At that moment Nic popped a champagne cork behind her and Sam jumped a mile high. Whirling to face him, she saw that he was so busy filling crystal flutes with the sparkling wine that he seemed oblivious to her. She was sure he had no idea how fast her heart was racing.

But then, as if suddenly aware of her, Nic looked up and grinned when he saw her watching him. Sam's stomach did an excited little somersault. He looked like a fallen angel—dark and dangerous and tempting.

Tempting in spite of her worry.

He'd tossed off his jacket and tie and rolled up his sleeves. He looked casual. Ever elegant. And sexy.

Nic walked toward her then, loose limbed and graceful. His cast was off, so he carried a flute in each hand. She started to walk toward him. "No, stay there," he said. "Standing there, with only the sky for a backdrop, you look like an angel." He reached her and handed her one of the flutes.

"You are innocence and temptation in one lovely package," he told her, then ran the knuckles of his free hand down her upper arm with its too well-defined biceps. "Power and softness."

Sam could only stare into his dark, deep-set eyes.

Then Nic clicked his flute to hers. "To excellent bargains," he said quietly. Quietly, because volume wasn't necessary when he stood so close.

Sam took a gulp of the champagne and tried to smile up at him. Then she was unable to look away again, even when Nic dipped his head and their lips met in a soft first kiss. Sam figured it was probably the best first kiss in history. At first, she even thought the champagne bubbles had gone right into her bloodstream and were exploding all through her.

Then he kissed her again. Firmer. Longer. And her eyelids closed of their own volition. He slid his fingertips along her jaw next, then cupped her face as he ran his tongue along the seam of her lips. It was instinct alone that told her to relax her jaw and grant him entry. But then she realized it wasn't her instincts at all. It was Nic. Somehow with one kiss he'd taken control of her body. And she didn't care. Then the explosions inside doubled, then tripled in intensity and frequency.

Nic broke the kiss and she realized she wasn't the only one having trouble with a thundering heart and breathing that was much too quick. "At first," he said next to her ear, "when I saw your hair up, I was disappointed. I have wanted to hold this spun gold in my hands, you see." His breath on her neck sent a wave of unnamed longing through her. "But then I realized I would be the one to take it down," he continued as he pulled a pin out of her hair and dropped it to the floor.

Then another.

And another.

Each pin, punctuated with a kiss or a nip on her neck, fueled a fire that went quickly from a warm glow to a raging blaze. Like the entire day, life blurred. In a fog of overloaded sensations and a deluge of stunning impressions, his hands and lips moved over her. And her worry over this new experience became a craving instead. She wanted him. Wanted to touch him. Feel his warm tanned skin under her hands.

Then she was floating as he swept her up in his arms and mounted the steps. Not once did his lips cease their assault on her senses. There was a sudden chill of air-conditioned air as her dress puddled around her, then there were cool, smooth sheets on her back as he caressed the rest of her body.

Nic was there then, warm and smooth, murmuring praises in his beautiful romantic native tongue. *Mia preziosa*—my precious—he called her. He thought she was beautiful. He liked her small, toned body. Could she have translated that right?

But then it didn't matter because that clever bilingual tongue laved her breasts and his firm lips were traversing her naked body, fanning the flames of desire higher. It was all like a dream—a beautiful, exciting dream. It was so like the dream she'd had at the start of this whirlwind week that the real felt unreal.

Then she reached out to touch him and Sam knew it was real. He was real. Hands roaming his shoulders, Sam found his hair and dragged him up, needing his lips on hers, needing his taste on her tongue.

But still she needed more.

Needed him closer. Inside her. And since Nic always seemed to know what she wanted—needed—he was there pressing into her. She gasped at a slight stinging pain that Nic echoed with a soft curse. He started to pull away but Sam wasn't giving him up. Not yet. She wrapped her legs around his waist and begged for more. She didn't know what she wanted, but she knew there had to be more than this aching need he'd created in her.

Nic fought to clear his head, to stop before he hurt her even more, but Samantha didn't seem to understand. She wrapped those wonderfully toned legs around him and drew him closer. "Please," she gasped. "Please don't leave me like this."

It flashed in his mind that leaving her was going to be nearly impossible now, but the thought drifted away. She had his head spinning too fast for thought. He'd only had a sip of champagne but just breathing in her scent was more intoxicating than the whole bottle could have been. Since Nic had denied her nothing from the moment they'd forged their friendship, he slid home again, claimed her lips and felt her explode around him.

And then, helpless, he joined her in the insanity of the moment. He felt as if his spirit had shattered in a million pieces only to reform, with him now a new man.

A man he didn't recognize.

And that terrified him as nothing in his life ever had—even imminent death. He lay there with Samantha cradled beneath him, feeling too damn much. Trying to grasp what exactly he did feel.

Then it came to him.

He felt betrayed.

This was supposed to be easy, casual sex with a friend. A bargain with mutual benefits. It was not supposed to be earth-shattering, life-altering lovemaking with an unforgettably sweet and sensual virgin.

The sudden need to flee, to deny what this had meant to him, overwhelmed Nic. He felt trapped but physically he wasn't. Samantha had gone limp, her breathing quiet and slow. Her eyes closed.

Looking down at her, he realized he was mesmerized by the sight of her. If he was trapped, it was by her loveliness. Because she was lovely and so much more. The trouble was that Samantha was more than he'd bargained for.

Nic forced himself to roll away, and his shoulder screamed. His physical agony seemed to reflect a sharper, more emotional pain.

"Where are you going, Nic?" Samantha asked sleepily as he moved away from the bed.

"Shower," he snapped.

Without a backward glance he stalked to the bathroom, stepped into the shower and twisted the handle sending icy water cascading over him. And again his shoulder protested sharply. Cursing quietly, he quickly fumbled with the hot tap until he was comfortable. He lathered up, hoping the soap would wash away her scent. He'd never be able to think straight if he didn't clear his senses of her.

She'd seduced him with that innocence of hers. That was what made her different. He'd assumed she was inexperienced but not entirely without experience, either. How could she have been chaste at twenty-seven? This was America. Having sex here was practically a rite of passage. Did anyone graduate high school here still a virgin? Possibly—but certainly not from college. He'd understood that dormitories were even coed, these days. How could the men on that campus have been so stupid as to let her get away? But they had and now Nic was left to deal with their stupidity.

Why was he so grateful to them at the same time?

He banished that question for one he'd rather explore. Why had Samantha not told him? Warned him? She had to have known how unusual she was. Had leaving him ignorant been some sort of a test? One he was bound to fail? No. That would have been stupid on her part since it was she he could have hurt—did hurt—more than necessary. Had she thought it wouldn't matter to him?

Or had she simply valued herself so little.

More than setting him up to fail, that infuriated him and it made the most sense. Damn her father. He'd certainly had a lot to answer to when he'd reached the Pearly Gates. Nic angrily twisted the tap off and strode back out of the shower, wrapping a towel around his waist as he moved back down the hall to the bedroom.

He stopped as he turned the corner to enter the bedroom, instantly remembering an American cartoon he'd once seen, in which the character had morphed into the shape of a heel. Nic had understood the imagery once he'd understood the meaning. Now, however, he understood the feeling.

Samantha was crying.

He'd made her cry.

Nic backed up into the hall and slumped against a wall out of her line of vision. He called himself every kind of a slimy toad, but it didn't help. Never had he cared if a woman cried, yet Samantha's quiet tears positively devastated him. His hand went to his chest and he rubbed the ache there. He really didn't want to know why he cared so much now.

Caring deeply for Samantha was not part of their bargain. She wanted a baby. He wanted offspring but wasn't father material. He was supposed to give her a child, and she was supposed to raise it and allow him a few visits.

Now, though, he wanted her more than he had any other woman. Her innocent response, strength and solid muscles were more alluring than all the practiced, reed-thin, angular women he'd known in the past. No wonder the others had never touched his heart. It was they and not Samantha who were not his type. He'd been smart enough to stay away from innocents until now. Worse, now that he'd held her, kissed her, made love with her, Nic was very afraid he wanted Samantha in his life forever.

But theirs was a temporary arrangement. His carefully orchestrated bargain. And it had just exploded in his face.

This was his fault and now he'd made her cry. He couldn't let her go on feeling whatever it was he'd made her feel. It wasn't her fault. He was the one wanting to change the rules, not Samantha. And he couldn't change the rules without the risk of hurting an innocent child.

He had no choice but to get a handle on this. Making love to her again was in no way going to make that easier. He would have to find a way to keep himself apart from her until he got his emotions under control.

Sam tried to stifle her tears. She never cried. Not before Nic had entered her life. Big deal that he hadn't stayed at her side and had sounded annoyed when she'd wanted to know where he was going. Wasn't it enough that he'd made her first sexual experience so wonderful? He'd taken a petrified lump of unkissed nerves and, with one touch, had somehow transformed her into a sensual network of wonderfully electrified nerve endings.

Her heart fell a little. Maybe he'd been annoyed because she'd disappointed him. Well, of course. That was it. It made perfect sense that she'd failed at this just the way she had at everything else to do with being a woman. He'd made love to the world's most beautiful and experienced women. She hadn't had a chance.

But, still, why was she crying as if her heart had broken? You'd think she'd be used to disappointing the people she loved.

Everything in her paused. Loved?

Could it be that she cared about Nic as more than just a friend and the future father of her baby? Had she begun to love him as her mother apparently thought? Sam held her breath. How would she have felt if, rather than merely leaving the room to take a shower, he'd been walking out of her life to go off and race those damn boats?

Dear God, she'd have been devastated. No. She *would* be devastated. Because that was exactly what he would do sooner or later. Their baby would give him his legacy. His piece of immortality. Then he'd be free to go out and risk his life.

Well, she couldn't let him know how she felt. That just wouldn't do. She wiped her tears again and stiffened her spine. Love and a clinging wife were not what Nic's bargain marriage was all about. It was about a mutually beneficial arrangement. And it was up to her to keep it that way.

Now, all she had to do was figure out how to hide her feelings. And that was going to take a little time. Time she might not have. She'd heard the shower go off a while ago. That meant Nic probably would be returning soon. Quickly, Sam hunkered down and pretended to sleep while thanking God Nic didn't know he'd made her cry. How would she have explained that?

Bottom line: She had a lot of thinking to do and even more to hide than a few dumb tears.

## Chapter Nine

In the morning, Nic ordered breakfast, then went up to the bedroom level to wake Samantha. He'd already found the nightgown and robe she'd packed in their combined overnight bag. He wanted her to have them immediately available in case she was embarrassed by her nudity. He had no experience with virgins—or at least virgins he'd recently deflowered—but he thought perhaps she'd have a stronger sense of modesty than the kind of women he was familiar with.

His plan had been to walk back into the room last night, wake her immediately and then leave, but the sight of her sleeping in the clear morning light of the desert held him transfixed. Her lips were swollen and her cheeks rosy. She looked like a woman who'd been thoroughly loved. And she had been. By him.

The trouble—though trouble was a rather poor choice of words—was that she'd been so responsive, so bold in her answering touches that never once had he suspected it was her first time. He'd been appalled later at how quickly he'd moved them from one stage of lovemaking to the next. He'd rushed her when, if he'd known, he would have taken his time, gone slowly to give her time to adjust to his touch. To his size and weight. He couldn't figure out why he hadn't scared her out of her mind.

The other problem was that, for him, last night had been a life-altering experience when all he'd expected was just another night in bed with a woman he happened to desire. That realization had made him nervous and testy afterward. He had never been so clumsy with a woman's feelings before but, perhaps, that was because, for the first time, his own feelings had been involved. Which was why there were tearstains on her face and why he was the clod who had put them there. He still hadn't decided if he should mention those tears.

Nic wondered if his indecision had anything to do with his mind-numbing exhaustion. He hadn't slept much, hauntingly conscious of her gloriously naked body on the other side of the bed. Never before had he been so tempted to awaken a woman with his lovemaking and not acted on the idea. Never before had he been afraid to.

And still, all his thinking and worrying had left him with only questions. Putting his own feelings aside, he had decided on one action. Nic knew he needed to explain his boorish behavior as he left their bed. What he planned to tell her was a bit of a lie, but it was one better told than omitted. Because he was very afraid her tears had been about the slant she'd put on his mood when he'd left their bed. Halfway through the night, he'd remembered something she'd said that day last Sunday when he'd found her in pain in the equipment shed. When she'd told him about the prognosis for her condition, she'd said she'd failed at everything to do with being a woman, even procreation.

All at once, her tears last night had made prefect sense. He'd nearly awakened her then but he'd opted for waiting till morning, hoping to eliminate the temptation of having her so near *and* awake. But morning was here and he couldn't allow her to go on thinking she'd failed him. Not when he would never be able to find her equal. Not when an act that had grown routine, though enjoyable, had blossomed into a life-changing event for him.

Nic took a deep breath and sank down next to her on the bed. Samantha's eyes popped open immediately. Confusion and then wariness crossed her face before she looked past him to the glass wall overlooking the rest of the loft, her expression carefully blank.

He winced, knowing he'd put that look there. He'd hurt her and it made him sick. Before last night, he'd never been able to read her expressions and now he wished he still couldn't. "I've ordered breakfast. It should be here in half an hour. Is that enough time for you to shower?" he asked, no longer hungry himself. "I hated to wake you but our flight is in a little less than three and a half hours."

She scooted up in bed to lean against the soft brown headboard, careful to keep herself covered. She'd been so open last night, so naturally bold. Now she seemed ashamed and self-conscious, not just modest. "I'm… uh…not used to running around naked."

"Your gown and robe are at the foot of the bed. I came to the conclusion that this was a new experience for you on my own. A man can tell, *mia preziosa*. I realized it a little late but I did realize. You should have told me."

She blushed but met his gaze. "I thought I had. I told you I don't date."

"I didn't realize you meant you never had. Ever. I'm sorry I hurt you."

"You didn't," she said quickly.

As much as he wanted to accept her denial, he knew it wasn't true. "Yes, I did and perhaps not only physically. I should have taken the time to explain why I rushed to the shower. I think, perhaps, you foolishly think I was fleeing you. I'm very afraid you think you disappointed me."

She rolled her eyes, her lips took on a sarcastic slant. "The thought had crossed my mind, Casanova. I think it happened somewhere between falling asleep in your arms and waking up to see your naked butt as you practically ran down the hall away from me. I didn't really think I could compete favorably with all your women, but a girl can't help dreaming."

"Ah. Direct as always." He smiled in spite of the seriousness of the subject. "I promise you, my testiness had nothing to do with you. Please blame my actions on my own injured machismo. I had thought to make love to you again to make up for my clumsiness the first time, but that was beyond the current ability of my shoulder. I strained it and needed to get it under the warm water. I promise I will be up to performing again, but not as soon as I should. I will keep up my end of our bargain as soon as my shoulder is up to the exercise."

She lobbed a soft punch to his good shoulder. "Yeah, well, carrying me up those stairs was a dumb stunt. I'm not surprised it's put you out of commission for a while." She grinned—no, really, it was more of a smirk—and said, "It was rather Prince Charming-esque of you, though. You really are a stud, huh?" she teased, lightening the moment with her own brand of sassy humor. "I finally understand why legions fall at your feet. Now, scat, so I can shower in peace."

Nic "scatted," a bit ashamed at his cowardice when Samantha was so refreshingly truthful and brave. But when had she ever not said what was on her mind? He wished in this instance, however, that his past had not formed her opinion of him. Because the number of women he'd been with no longer felt like a matter of pride. And he didn't want Samantha remembering it at every turn.

Feeling as if she'd been given a reprieve, Sam had been only too happy to assure Nic that the night before had been anything but a disappointment. Nic was used to casual sex so she was nearly sure compliments were okay. After all, if it wasn't enjoyable, why would you do something so intimate in the first place?

Sam was sorry he'd hurt himself on her account, especially since his pain gave her the time she needed to think her way through her feelings for him. And that made her feel guilty as hell.

What would solve her problem was to find out she was already pregnant. That way, she wouldn't have to risk making love with him again. The bond between them had grown stronger since yesterday and she knew it had to be their lovemaking that had strengthened it. How much stronger would it grow if they made love again? Often?

The resulting heartbreak was too painful to contemplate.

Once the sex thing was out of the way, they were able to chat at breakfast about other things like the grapes, a few of Nic's ideas to rescue the crop and how to get Juliana to bring Will back as vintner. Nic felt that was crucial to their prosperity.

On the plane they discussed a strategy for explaining his offer to pay off the loan. Nic suggested they wait until she was pregnant. Then he planned to play an overbearing Italian husband to the hilt. He'd storm on about how worried she was about those payments and what Harley Bryant would do next to sabotage their efforts to grow the business. He would explain that he didn't want his wife worrying so much in her delicate condition.

Sam laughed and said there was never going to be anything delicate about her. That was the only time Nic slipped into being the way he'd been at the Skyloft. He took her hand and kissed the back of it. When she looked up into his eyes, he held her gaze by the sheer magnetism of his will. Then he said, in a terribly serious tone, "You are either in terrible need of glasses or you need a new mirror in your room."

As in Las Vegas, Nic had a limo waiting at Philly International to take them to Hopetown. Sam wasn't as much impressed with the luxury as she was with the efficiency and ease of the arrangements he'd made.

They were both silent during the forty-five-minute drive, as if they'd both run out of the small talk they'd begun using to avoid tougher, more important topics they needed to discuss.

When Nic and Sam arrived home, they expected a nice family celebration. And they got that. Juliana had the dining room set for a lovely family luncheon and there was even a small two-tier wedding cake. There was also a surprise that was both unexpected and unwelcome.

One of the important items they'd avoided talking about was their new sleeping arrangements at Hopewell Manor. For some reason, they both thought they'd be able to retreat to their separate quarters. That would give them time for their mutual but unexpressed need to ponder the dilemma of actually being in love with their temporary spouse. The family had other quite natural ideas on the subject of accommodations that didn't fit with that scenario.

Nic had moved toward the main stairs after Abby, Caro and Trey returned to work. He planned to take their shared overnighter upstairs when Juliana called out, "Wait, Niccolò. Bring that this way. Both of you, come, follow me. We have a surprise."

Sam's stomach fell, and she stared at Nic, whose expression had turned confused. She put it all together quickly, then it looked as if Nic had, too, but his expression returned to neutral so quickly she wasn't sure if he'd looked alarmed or not.

At the end of the long hall built entirely of glass so it resembled an old-fashioned conservatory sat the newest addition to the manor. Juliana stepped aside just inside and motioned them ahead. The addition boasted a large sitting room with a cathedral ceiling and circular stairs that led to a new bedroom and bath. It was actually quite a lot like the Skyloft had been, except it was decorated in a classic Colonial style with a little Tuscan influence thrown in. Both levels had fireplaces and there was a full bath on each level, as well.

"We moved you both in so you have nothing to do but relax," Juliana explained. "Caroline and Trey rushed their move into their new house so you two could have this."

There was no way to refuse it, of course. But Sam tried. "Mama, this was your room. You were supposed to take it back when Caro and Trey moved out."

"Zia Juliana, I cannot take your room," Nic protested. "It's too much. I would never think to take—"

Juliana held up her hands halting his objection. "I don't want the room. There are too many memories in here. I like the room I have now. It's just the right size for one person. This was built for a couple."

Just as Juliana walked to the French doors and threw them open, Sam noticed the two chaises in the brick courtyard beyond the French doors. Between them sat a table with a decanter of wine and two glasses. It looked awfully romantic.

"Dinner at seven," Juliana said with a conspiratorial smile. "In the meantime, you two have a glass of vino. And relax. Unwind."

"But we were to check on the grapes. Samantha has been worried about the botrytis we noticed Friday," Nic objected.

Juliana smacked her forehead lightly. "Oh. I completely forgot your messages. Sammy, honey, you had a call from one of your old professors. He said you'd called about that. He had some free time so he came over late yesterday. He thinks it's good news. He says it looks to him to be a form that will produce a nice sauterne style or the Late Harvest Johannesburg Riesling Nic mentioned. We've never done a dessert wine. That could be great fun. He took samples and promised to call you soon."

"Mama, we've never produced either. I'm not even sure I know how."

"I thought of that," she said with a careless flip of her wrist. "I contacted a vintner from the old country who was a great friend of my father's. He's retired now, but he's going to come here for an extended vacation and be this year's guest vintner. Next year, if you still don't feel ready to take over that aspect of Will's job, we'll find another. Isn't that an interesting concept?"

What had happened to her rock-solid mother? Guest vintners? "It's an interesting concept," Sam said, "but I'd still rather Will come back."

"Well, I wouldn't. Nic, I have a message for you. Your sister called." Juliana walked to the sofa table and picked up a message. "I wrote it down. She said congratulations on the wedding. That she concedes the check to you but she has a year to think of her next move. Does that make sense?"

Nic took the message, reread it, then balled it up in his fist. Sam hadn't thought Nic's sister would openly show her hostility this way. She hoped Nic could deflect her mother's curiosity about the cryptic message that had meaning only if you knew about their bargain and the terms of his grandfather's will.

"This is typical of my sister," he said disgustedly. "Our relationship is strained, at best. I simply ignore her like the pest she is."

Juliana shrugged and dismissed the message as easily as Nic seemed to. "Whatever you say, Niccolò. Now Mama's orders are that you two are to do nothing today but get used to being a married couple."

"But—" Sam began.

Nic stepped in cutting off Sam's protests. "Thank you, Zia. I find getting Samantha to relax is a difficult task, but I will throw myself into it with my whole being."

Her mother laughed and floated out of the room. "I just bet you will," she quipped over her shoulder, and shut the door behind her as she stepped into the hall.

"Nic! What will Mama think?"

Nic laughed. "She will think we had only a twelve-hour honeymoon and that I am grateful for even this short extension to it. I have an image to protect," he said lightly, then sobered. "And so do you. Do you want them to know you don't love me as they think you do?"

Sam stared at him. Why did he sound annoyed? "No more than you want them or your sister to know you don't love me," she answered truthfully. It even hurt to say it and that made her more restless. She walked into the courtyard and picked up a glass.

Turning back to Nic, she said, "So let's have a little wine, enjoy the breeze and sunshine and maybe catnap in the chaises. My body is totally confused about what time it is."

Thinking his body had other things on its mind than time, Nic walked out into the brick courtyard. He hadn't ventured into this part of the house because it had been Caroline and Trey Westerly's sanctuary. The courtyard was entirely enclosed on all sides with tall stone walls. It looked like a secret garden. Pots overflowed with flowers. Clematis and climbing roses grew on trellises attached to the walls and impatiens grew in lavish profusion filling the raised beds at the foundation of the addition. There was even a fountain bubbling on the wall opposite the French doors.

When he glanced back at the main house, he noticed that none of the windows in the house looked out onto this courtyard. He wasn't sure if he was more relieved that no one could see them simply sitting in separated chaises or more tempted to share a chaise and take advantage of the complete privacy.

Nic had a sudden vision of Samantha and him naked and entwined on the grapevine-patterned cushions. He forced the image away and studiously avoided looking at Samantha as he poured them both a glass of the private reserve chardonnay Zia had left decanted and breathing for them. Nic sat down and closed his eyes pretending to drift off as Samantha joined him on the patio. But his sleeplessness the night before had taken its toll and soon playacting was fact.

The courtyard became his refuge in the next two weeks. He'd sit out there reading by torchlight—not an easy feat—until he was sure she'd fallen asleep. Then he'd go to bed but the waiting didn't keep him safe from temptation. Almost every night he'd awaken in the early hours of the new day to find her in his arms, her hair soft as silk and smelling like honey and melons. One of her strong arms was often wrapped around his middle and often a long shapely leg was tangled with his.

In the moonlight that illuminated their bed through the glass panes of the palladium windows above the French doors to the courtyard, he'd watch her sleeping and fight the temptation to kiss her lips until they were as swollen as they'd been the first morning of their marriage. So far, he'd fought the urge to steep himself in the feel of her, knowing Samantha wouldn't welcome the feelings that went along with his burning desire. He didn't welcome them, either.

He didn't know how much longer he could stand his self-imposed isolation from her. Nor what good it was doing, anyway. But, there he was, spending the end of another evening icing his shoulder after doing his exercises. He honestly didn't know why he was working so hard to get in the kind of shape he needed to be in for racing. He didn't even want to go back on the circuit. But, of course, he had to. After Samantha gave birth, he had to be gone so he wouldn't chance emotionally scarring their child.

Lightning suddenly lit up the sky and a crack of thunder clapped almost immediately. The rain started next, and Nic jumped up and ran inside the room. And for the second time in their short marriage, Nic found Samantha crying as if her heart had broken. This time she was curled up in the corner of the sitting room sofa.

His first thought was, what had he done now?

The last time he'd taken the coward's way out and had retreated rather than confront her. This time he had no choice because he'd made such a racket tearing into the room that she now sat staring up at him. The surprised look in her widened eyes told him she'd forgotten he was just outside the closed French doors. He tossed his book and ice packs on a chair and rushed to her.

"*Mia preziosa,* what is wrong?" he crooned, unwilling to let her pretend nothing was.

"It didn't work," she said, her arms folded across her middle. She was clearly in great pain. Then, like the day he'd found her in the equipment shed, she pressed her forehead against her bent knees and fell silent, hiding her face.

Confused, he asked, "What didn't work?"

She looked up, her gaze accusing. "The...the sex in Vegas. It didn't work."

Was she feeling the strain he was? Or did she still think she'd failed him that night. The latter was more likely.

"I thought you understood. I hurt my shoulder with too much activity. You, in no way, failed me that night."

"No, I failed me—us. After all, you want…a baby, too." A heartbreaking sob whispered from her throat and quaked through her small compact body. "I'm not pregnant. We did it at the perfect…time in my cycle… but I couldn't even do that…right. Thousands of women get…pregnant by accident… I can't even do it…on purpose."

Nic hated more than anything her skewed perception of herself as a failure. He ran his hand over her slightly hunched back. And now that Caroline and Trey had announced a child on the way, she must be doubly upset. He had seen the look of hope in Samantha's eyes while they'd told the family. She'd hoped to be making the same announcement soon.

"I will hear no more of this talk of failure. We…" He hesitated. He would not call what they'd had together sex. He couldn't. He would call it what it had been for him and hope she'd think he was only using it as a euphemism. "We made love only once, Samantha. You are asking for one of the greatest miracles in nature. It's possible that earlier in your cycle or later would be what it takes for you. Many women who are trying to have a child fail the first month they try. And we only tried once in that month. We must just try more often.

"I blame myself. I didn't keep up my end of our bargain. I was a…a big baby about my shoulder," he lied, then with a pang of guilt for the greatest lie of all, he added, with a teasing note to his voice, "We must get with the program, no? I grow anxious to return to my team."

He didn't bother to add that he wasn't at all sure he'd be racing or just directing strategy and working with his mechanics on the boats. She wouldn't care. She just wanted her baby, him gone and not interfering in the rearing of their child. And once there was a child involved he would need to leave.

Disloyal though it was, Nic was glad there was no child yet. It gave him time to be with her. Even though he'd kept to himself, his love still grew each day. He would be a fool not to spend every moment with her that he could. He'd memorize each smile, each saucy rebuttal, each beautiful sigh for the lonely days he'd wander with his team, wishing for his home.

He brightened a little. Perhaps, he'd spend holidays here. Come for birthdays and not just send gifts. Get to see her with their child, both happy and content and safe from his constant influence but better for his once having been in their lives. It wasn't much but it would have to be enough.

Nic took her chin, still buried behind her upraised knees and made her look at him. "Have you taken something for the pain? Uh-uh. No denying that you are in pain. I am no fool. I keep telling you how much I know of women."

Deep color invaded her creamy complexion. "I took

something already, okay?" she snarled with disgust rife in her tone as she pulled away from him to wipe her eyes. Never had he seen a woman so disgusted with her own frailty. Usually they used their tears and fragility to their advantage. That was why Samantha was so refreshingly wonderful.

Already showered and ready for bed, Nic took her hand and pulled her to her feet. "Come. It's time for us to act like friends and not strangers."

"But, Nic, I'm really not up to—"

"My friend is sad and I want to hold her. Is there anything wrong with that?" When she shook her head, he led her to the circular stairs and followed her up. He sauntered to the bed, slid under the covers and held out his arms. "Come," he ordered.

"I'm sorry for the waterworks." She sniffled as she walked toward him. "I'm an idiot. You should just ignore me."

When she climbed in next to him, Nic pulled her against his chest. "You are a sweet woman who is disappointed. But we will work to make sure you are not disappointed again. Now I will rub your back the way my *nonna* used to rub mine when I was upset by Gina or my father, and you will be asleep in no time at all. Is it not an American saying that everything always looks better in the morning?"

## Chapter Ten

The next morning, Sam woke in Nic's arms and that alone made everything better. She still didn't know how she was going to handle it when he left, but before she fell asleep last night, with his hand gently stroking her back, she came to a decision. She would enjoy him to the fullest while she could.

While she had him.

She loved him. She loved everything about him—especially the way he'd made her feel in Las Vegas. She even loved his fabricated playboy image now that she was in on the joke.

It couldn't hurt less to watch him leave than it did to be so close and yet so far. She regretted every second she'd wasted from the two weeks since that incredible night in the Las Vegas Skyloft all the way back to the moment she met him and dismissed him as beneath her notice.

Not for the first time since getting to know Nic, Sam wondered how she could have been so dumb as to judge a whole half of the human race so harshly because of three men. Lying there in Nic's arms a fog lifted from her mind like the curtain of a stage.

It had only been three men.

Three!

Her grandfather had been stiff, overbearing and cold. He'd never spoken a word to Sam that hadn't been a criticism of some type. From her dress being wrinkled, to her face being dirty, to her hair being too short. She'd never been good enough to be his granddaughter.

Her father had been so self-centered that he hadn't cared about her and her sisters or even their mother, except how their looks and behavior reflected on him. He had been hypercritical of Sam, just like his father. She hadn't projected the image of the Hopewell family he wanted portrayed. And he'd been hypocritical, as well, considering the scandalous way he ended his marriage to her mother.

At the same time there'd been Kyle Winston, Caro's fiancé. Sam had nurtured a tremendous crush on him in the way younger sisters often adored their older sister's boyfriend. He'd broken his engagement to Caro because of her parents' very public breakup. Kyle had claimed to be unable to live in the shadow of the scandal.

And James Hopewell had certainly created a local scandal. He'd slept with, impregnated and then married his young intern, with the marriage taking place just after his divorce from Juliana.

Sam's reaction to the events of that year had been to write off the rest of the men on the planet right along with Kyle, her father and her grandfather.

It had taken Nic to prove to her that there were good men in the world besides Will, her mother's would-be suitor. She'd been lucky enough to find Nic and she'd wasted so much of her time with him. Idiot!

Caroline had even caught her hiding from Nic last week. Talk about embarrassing! Sam had used the excuse that she was all muddy and didn't want him seeing her like that. It was true enough, but fear of the heartbreak to come had been the real reason.

Caro had stepped back and shaken her head as she'd assessed Sam's appearance. "Forget the mud," she'd quipped. "It's the least of your problems. Why do you wear everything two sizes too big? Don't you get sick of pulling your belt that tight just to keep your pants from falling down?"

"My clothes are comfortable," she'd countered, and crossed her arms under her too ample breasts. "And I doubt they're two sizes too big."

"Your clothes are tents," had been Caro's snippy rejoinder. "You've married a world-class hunk. I think you can safely stop hiding your light under a bushel, little sister. I've seen the way he looks at you. Believe me, he's seen it shining, anyway. It wasn't your clothes that kept men at bay, anyway. It was the poisonous darts you practically shot at any man who got within range."

Though she thought the metaphor was a bit extreme, Sam had admitted to herself that her sister was right about her clothes and her prickliness. So she'd gone to the new consignment shop in town to see if she could find some work jeans in a smaller size and a few serviceable T-shirts to go along with them.

The simple shopping trip into town proved to be something Sam had never before experienced. The only occasion that had come close was the day in Vegas when Nic had turned her over to the woman at the hotel and told her to outfit Sam from the skin out for their private wedding.

Unlike that day, this shopping trip had turned into a world-class spree. Your Sister's Closet was the name of the cute new consignment shop. It was owned by an entrepreneurial thirtysomething young woman who'd seen Sam as a blank canvas. That's exactly what she'd been. The blank canvas, however, was two sizes smaller, as Caro had said, and than Sam, with all her heart, had previously believed herself to be.

As she'd hauled bag after bag of clothes to her truck, Sam had decided shopping could be fun. Never more so than nearly a week later when she arrived on the stone patio off the kitchen for an alfresco dinner. Nic choked on his wine after catching sight of her in the blue sundress Sarah Canfield had all but forced her to try on. Watching his eyes go two shades darker as he stood and stared down at her had Sam deciding that the proprietor of the town's newest shop just might be her new best friend.

Nic pulled out a chair for her without looking away, then bent and kissed her neck as she settled on the wrought iron chair next to him. Sam hoped and prayed he'd ask her about making love again so she didn't have to ask him. She wasn't sure if her new clothes gave her that much courage.

"You look lovely, *cara,*" he whispered, and then sat and stared at her for long moments with a definite promise gleaming in his eyes.

Everyone had just about finished eating dinner—a dinner she scarcely remembered—when Nic said, "Your shopping expedition last week certainly went well." He snapped his fingers with a slight grimace on his handsome face. "I am an ungrateful fool. I never told you how much I enjoyed that legal thriller you bought me that day. I found myself hooked from the first sentence to the last."

"I guess, that's why it's on the bestseller list. You read so much I just naturally thought of you when I heard it advertised."

"I'd never have pegged you as a big reader, Nic," Abby commented.

"I never was before the accident. Since then, I've found the more I read in English, the better I think in English. It helps develop my vocabulary and a better understanding of American idioms, as well. Though I hate to spoil all of Samantha's fun. She is often amused at my expense."

Forgetting about her mother and Abby because she only had eyes for Nic most of the time, Sam remarked, "If you're working this hard on your English, does that mean you plan to stay here in the States, for the most part?"

Nic blinked then frowned. He glanced sideways at Abby and her mother, making Sam realize how huge a mistake she'd just made. "I wouldn't think of dragging you away from your family and the vineyard you love so much," he scolded. "Why would you think such a thing of me? There really is nothing in Italy for me now but Nonna. Much as I love her, she will not live for many more years. She is over eighty now."

"Considering the press your simple wedding got, I thought you and Nic would have talked about where you're going to live before this," Abby said, her gaze jumping from Nic to her and back again in amazement. "Suppose you each gave a reporter a different answer. Just what we don't need is the Hopewell name plastered in the tabloids again. I can see it now. 'Samantha Verdini won't leave her mama. Is this the end of the honeymoon?'"

Sam eyed Abby. Like their father and grandparents, Abby was too wrapped up in the family name. She worried about it so much it stifled any other reaction she might have.

Juliana reached out, touched Abby's hand, chuckling lightly. "Darling, love is often all a couple thinks about at first. Whether there are reporters asking questions or not, Nic and Sammy are just a young couple in love. I didn't care where your father lived. I'd have married him if he'd lived on the dark side of the moon. He was all I needed. I left Italy without looking back. I'm sure Sammy was merely willing to go wherever Niccolò is. And apparently Nic feels the same way."

Abby looked a little confused. Suddenly, so was Sam.

She'd always imagined their mother had felt like a fish out of water when she first arrived in Hopetown. She'd imagined a sad, homesick woman-child all alone in a big foreign world with Sam and her sisters' high-society grandparents picking at her every chance they got.

All three of the sisters had assumed their grandparents had simply overpowered the young girl Juliana had been with their flagrant disapproval. The sisters had seen Juliana as having been forced into the image of the perfect Americanized wife for the scion of the historically prominent Hopewell family. Sam had thought their father had abandoned their mother to the elder Hopewells' manipulations only to ultimately reject the product they'd created for him when he'd turned to a younger woman.

"Mama," Abby said, trying to get her mother's attention. But Juliana was staring off over the river, deep in thought.

"*Cara,* shall we walk along the river and let our dinner settle?" Nic said.

"As soon as I help Abby clear the table for Hannah," she promised, anxious to be alone with Nic.

"You two go for your walk." Abby stood, waved them off and started collecting dishes. "I'm sorry I jumped all over you. Would you like me to tell Hannah you'll have your dessert in your suite?"

"That'd be great, Ab," Sam told her.

"Is the courtyard okay?" Abby asked.

Sam nodded. "And would you ask her to decant some of that '99 chardonnay Nic likes so much?"

Nic took her hand, calling Sam's attention to him. He looked unsettled. "You remembered I like the '99 chardonnay? *Grazie, cara.* Thank you." Then he kissed the back of the hand he held and pulled her to her feet. He led the way down the stone steps to the expansive lawn. They strolled hand in hand to the river's edge.

Sam didn't quite understand why Nic was so affected because she remembered something as inconsequential as his preference in wine. It seemed only natural to her, so she asked why it didn't to him.

Nic stared at her for a long moment, then he smiled as he shook his head. "You brought home that book for me. You helped Hannah bring our dinner to the courtyard the night I was in so much pain after my therapy appointment. You made sure my shoulder was packed in ice before you would even eat. These things don't seem extraordinary to you?"

Sam shrugged. She had done all of those things because Nic was such a sweet guy. It felt natural to reciprocate his kindnesses with her own. She loved him. She wanted him to be as happy as he could be while languishing in Hopetown as he tried to give her the child that had been her lifelong dream—someone who would love her for herself.

He was doing so much for her. Had already done so much for her. Sam felt as if he'd opened up a new world for her to see. Because of him, when she looked in the mirror, she saw a new woman.

That was how she felt. New.

That he was so affected by a few simple kindnesses

got her thinking. It was as if she'd managed to touch his heart without meaning to. Maybe, with enough time, he'd come to feel a modicum of the love for her that she felt for him. Maybe then he wouldn't leave her to rush off to his old life—his old dangerous life.

Reality reared its head. *Yeah, Sam, and maybe there's a Santa Claus, a tooth fairy and an Easter Bunny. Get real. Like a few books and ice packs will make him love you. You may look better but you're still no Miss Universe.*

Nic stood by the river holding Samantha's hand, their fingers entwined. "You continue to surprise me," he told her, still bowled over by the change in her this last week. It had begun after he'd stopped hiding from her. Suddenly her mode of dress changed. Everything she wore now fit that beautiful body he'd uncovered in Las Vegas. Even her standard work uniform had evolved. Her jeans now lovingly hugged her bottom and her T-shirts were actually cut for a woman with little extra touches of femininity. After a shower she often changed into something a little nicer for dinner, though she was usually still dressed casually.

But this dress she wore now had set him on fire the moment he'd seen her. Thin little straps held up a bodice that gave him quite a view of the breasts he longed to caress once again. It had a full skirt and was made of what looked like silk. He doubted it could feel as soft and silky as the body it covered, but he longed to touch it anyway. To fill his hands with the material as he pulled her against his aching groin.

She seemed pleased as a sly little smile tipped her lips at the corners of her very kissable mouth. "Is it good that I surprise you?" she asked in a low, provocative tone. Having Samantha hone her sexual skills on him was amazingly arousing. And fulfilling. It kindled a fire within him that only she would ever be able to extinguish.

If nothing else, he had given her this.

Inflamed by just the thought of holding her, Nic wrapped his arm around her waist and pulled her closer. *Dio,* she felt so good against him. This time he nipped at her hand. "I am a very needy man just now. It may not be wise to tease me."

She grinned up at him, mischievous and adorably smug. "Am I teasing you?"

Though he loved seeing her so lighthearted, he could find nothing to joke about. "Only if you tell me you are still too indisposed to make love."

A little frown creased her usually smooth forehead. "I'm not, but I don't think the timing is right for me to get pregnant."

He was able to chuckle in his agony. "As if I care just now. Remember, practice makes perfect, *cara,*" Nic whispered, and let go of her hand so he could lean down and nip at her shoulder.

"You're just a font of old adages these days, aren't you?"

"The thing with old adages is that they became popular because of how often they are true." He nipped at her earlobe next and then sucked on it, laving it with his tongue. It was so satisfying to feel a shiver move through her body. He wasn't the only one in need, it would seem.

"I intend for us to practice. Much," he whispered in a voice gone rough with need and desire. He traced her spine with his fingertips down to her nicely round bottom and then guided her closer, pressing her against his groin. "Believe me when I say what we found together in Vegas was quite remarkable. Perhaps even magical. I think we should practice and perfect the magic. Come. I have pictured you naked under the stars on one of the chaises in our lovely private courtyard since I first saw it."

Samantha stepped out of his arms and tilted her head as she considered him. "It's funny you'd say that. I had a similar vision." She paused, then pressed her index finger against his chest and ran it to his belt buckle before adding, "A vision of you waiting there for me."

She pivoted then and ran toward the gate into their very private courtyard. Nic wasted no time catching up to her. They left each other's clothing strewn on the pathway through their secret garden. Luckily, the wine and dessert were already there so there was no danger of being interrupted. But it wouldn't have mattered to him if Hannah had forgotten the two of them completely.

Samantha was sweeter than any cake and more intoxicating than any wine. He'd never get enough of her, but he'd have to make do with what he could have now and the memories of her, later. For him, there was no other choice.

## Chapter Eleven

Two months later, Nic had decided *magic* was too tame a word to describe what there was between him and Samantha. Sorcery, perhaps. He smiled and inhaled the sweet musky scent of sex. Maybe it was witchcraft. That was it. She'd bewitched him. One smile from her and he wanted her. One come-hither look in her smoky hazel eyes and his legs trembled like a babe standing for the first time.

His love for her grew each day. But, each time he felt those inappropriate emotions, he reminded them both in one way or another that he was there only temporarily. Now, as with every night in the aftermath of their lovemaking, Samantha lay in his arms tempting him to want what he couldn't have.

"Perhaps this was the time, *cara*."

"Every time's so special," she said, whirling a finger in his chest hair, tracing some imaginary pattern. "It doesn't matter when, does it?"

"Not as long as it happens. Pleasant though our love-making is, my team grows anxious for my return to them—as do I," he lied, then added, "In fact, I must go to Seattle for the weekend. Jake is having a problem with the number two boat. He needs me to take it out and see what I think is wrong."

She sat up and even in the moonlight he saw her sudden pallor. "In a race? You can't race. You aren't ready! What are you going to do? Go out and get yourself killed just to please your teammate?"

"I have obligations other than our bargain, Samantha," he countered, hating himself but needing to get away to clear his head of her. Her simplest touch sent tentacles of need growing through him just as she wanted their child growing inside her.

Samantha rolled away and stood over their bed, glorious in her nakedness. Hands propped on her hips, hair shining silver and gold in the moonlight, she glared. "You're not obligated to kill yourself just to figure out what's wrong with a stupid boat."

"Do you have any idea what that stupid boat is worth? Each race Jake fails to win or even place in costs me money."

"In a year you'll have two million more from your grandfather's estate."

"I have to go. I have no choice. Jake says the engine

is cutting out at high speeds. That is dangerous for him." His hands itched to reach for her, but he fought the urge even though she was glorious standing there defending her position.

"Then, at least, don't drive that boat."

"I must. To duplicate what is happening, I must. Don't tell me how to do my job, Samantha! Our bargain doesn't give you the right."

"I'm sick to death of hearing about our bargain! Our bargain isn't supposed to include me attending your funeral."

When he caught the shimmer of a tear on her cheek, his next volley froze in his throat. She was only worrying about him. Not trying to control him, he assured himself. He rolled to his feet and moved toward her, aroused from seeing her lovely body shining in the moonlight. His heart ached with love just knowing she cared so much for his welfare. "We need not fight about this," he told her and knew she'd noticed his obvious condition.

"We need to if you're running in that race," she grumbled, and turned away from him.

Nic told himself the constriction in his chest was not due to feeling trapped but because of her obvious fear for him. Still, he couldn't let her control him with emotional blackmail as his grandfather had tried to do from the grave. But he also couldn't pretend she was using trickery. Samantha was too honest and forthright to be sneaky. She had come right out with her fears and worries.

Thinking of her many burdens, he hated knowing that he was adding to them. He vowed he'd pay off the loan in the morning and take away a worry since he'd added one. He would quietly confide to Zia Juliana that they wanted a child but were not having success. He'd explain about Samantha's condition and that they didn't want to delay having a family for fear her problems could escalate, making conception even more difficult later. He'd say they had been advised to remove worry from Samantha's life and to him that meant the loan and Harley Bryant. Then he'd hand Zia the paid-off mortgage. It wasn't the best timing for him financially, what with the problem Jake was having with the new engine, but that couldn't be helped.

Nothing mattered more to Nic than this child they were trying to create except its extraordinary mother. He stepped up behind her, his arousal blatant against her bottom and nuzzled her neck. "I'll take the boat out before the trials. I'll have Jake do the driving. Maybe that's the best way to shake the bugs out of it anyway, okay? It will just be Jake, me, the boat and the water. I promise not to let anyone talk me into getting behind the wheel or even participating in a race as a copilot."

He turned her into his arms, lifted her and she curled her legs about his waist as he entered her. "Nothing will stop me from creating our baby with you. Nothing is more important to me," he whispered, his throat aching to say more. His shoulder protested then and he sank to the bed with her flowing over him.

He looked up at Samantha. At her wild hair. At her lovely full breasts. And his senses caught fire. Together he and Samantha caught fire. Then he watched her almost from outside himself as he tucked away yet another beautiful memory of her throwing her head back as the orgasm took her. Quaking, she fell to his chest and he followed her over the edge of sanity. He nearly screamed out his love for her but managed to swallow the words he longed to say.

Making up had never been so fulfilling, Nic thought before he realized that it was tears and not sweat that tracked over his chest. And it was tears that ran into his hair from his own eyes, as well. He refused to consider what either of their tears meant. Heartbreak and happiness seemed always to taunt him. Which, he wondered, would be the last emotion he felt?

Sam winced when the morning light blasted into the bedroom. Her eyes popped back open in shock. She'd forgotten to close the drapes! She bounded out of bed as stealthily as she could and rushed to pick up the remote for the traverse rod to the floor-to-ceiling drapes that covered the palladium windows and the French doors below. She breathed a silent sigh when they'd quietly glided closed over the windows.

And her stomach turned over.

Sam looked back at Nic, still blissfully asleep, thank God. She wished she had time to just stand there and enjoy the view, but instead she rushed down the stairs toward the lower bathroom. Halfway there, her stomach started to heave. She tried to muffle the sound that had escaped her throat with her hands. Praying she hadn't awakened Nic, she rushed to the commode to complete what had become a new morning ritual.

The trouble was, in the last week it had escalated into a morning, noon and early evening occurrence. If this kept up, she wouldn't be able to keep her pregnancy a secret from Nic much longer. And she wasn't ready for him to know. Especially after he mentioned going to Seattle to help solve the problem with his boat.

She kept trying to weave a web of love about Nic, hoping that the happier he was, the more chance there was that he would come to love her as she loved him. That he would stay once their damn bargain was fulfilled. She loved her child but hated the bargain that would take Nic away from them. She longed to tell Nic how grateful she was for the child who had made his or her presence known almost from the first, but she was afraid to tell him. Afraid he'd leave.

She stood and wiped her mouth, then turned and gasped. Nic stood leaning lazily against the doorjamb. "How long were you going to wait to tell me?"

"Nic, I…" she began, wanting to pretend she wasn't sure, that this was the first day she'd gotten sick. But she couldn't lie. She knew the truth was written on her face, as usual.

She knew especially when he said, "Perhaps the better question is, how long *have* you waited?"

She sighed and sank to the edge of the big garden tub. "I think I'm about seven or eight weeks along."

He blinked. "Then, you lied about being irregular when I asked you last month. Why the charade?"

She longed to tell him how much she loved him, but hating the bargain anew, she thought that would be the dumbest thing she could say. Nic had never wanted her love. "Because I didn't want you to leave. God, Nic, I can't stand the thought of you in another accident. I thought, if you didn't know, you'd stay here trying to get me pregnant and you'd be safe for a while longer."

His dark eyes flared with anger and she realized her mistake. Nic hated being manipulated even when the manipulation had come from beyond the grave through the will of his much loved *nonno*. Nic was still furious three years later.

"A caged bird often flies away when he gets loose. They prefer to risk death rather than to live in captivity. I suppose I won't need to return from Seattle now that I've fulfilled my part of our bargain. Since you broke the first part of our bargain with your silence, I hope you keep the second part. I'll let you know where I am so you can inform me of the birth."

Nothing had ever hurt as much as his disappointment with her. Her whole world had come to an end in one horrible moment. "Please, Nic, I love you. I was just so afraid to lose you."

His eyes went colder and she hadn't thought that was possible. "Love? So you tried to force me to do what you wanted just like everyone else who has ever claimed to love me. I prefer honesty. It is what I foolishly believed I had found in you. But you lied and manipulated just like the rest of them."

"Nic," she cried, and reached for him, "please forgive me. I meant no harm."

His eyes narrowed and he took a step back, evading her hand as if he couldn't bear to have her touch him. Then he just looked terribly sad. "Why then, *cara,* do I feel so wounded?" he said, and turned away.

Sam was sure she'd never forget the look of desolation in his dark eyes. He looked as if he'd lost his last friend. She raised her eyes to gaze in the mirror across from the tub. Through a sheen of tears, she realized she looked exactly the same.

She'd lost her friend, and it hurt more than losing her lover.

Sam didn't know how Nic managed to leave without seeing anyone in the family, but he had. That left Sam to explain what had happened. She simply said he'd had to return to his team for financial reasons. But she knew everyone surmised that something had gone wrong, especially when she had to tell them she was pregnant.

She'd had no choice because she wasn't having an easy time of it. She was sick all the time. Sam loved her child fiercely—more so because the baby was a part of Nic she would have forever.

There was a silver lining to the cloud that hung over her, and that was that Will was back. Juliana had called him within a week of Nic's departure because Sam had fainted in a field and Jamie'd found her. Her nephew hadn't been the only one terrified. Her mother had called Will for help and he'd been there the next day.

Nic hadn't come home for Christmas. He was in Australia and his team was in a huge Christmas day race. He'd called but he'd been distant. With some flat ginger ale and a boatload of tears, Sam rang in the new year alone standing in the middle of the chilly courtyard where she thought her baby had been conceived.

Now Sam sat looking out at the snowy courtyard. February had roared in with a blizzard in the first week, and the snow still hadn't melted ten days afterward. For some reason, her nausea had returned. She'd tried to take her mind off it by reading, but the pages of her book kept blurring and then a headache blazed to life.

Sam put her feet up and noticed they were even more swollen today than yesterday. Feeling like a beached whale, she told herself she was glad Nic couldn't see her. But it was a lie. Her heart ached for the sight of him. She spent too much time with her heart in her mouth watching the sports channels trying to catch just a glimpse of him. And, when she did, he was usually either climbing into his boat in preparation for a race or accepting a trophy. It was hard not to be proud even as her heart was pounding with fear for him. He was ahead in the World Cup, but was it wishful thinking that his smiles for the cameras never looked quite genuine?

She felt like a fraud staying there in the master suite. They all thought Nic would be back. But Sam knew better. Her mother had a better chance of accepting Will into her life and using this master suite with him than Sam did of ever having Nic there with her again. Winning the World Cup could hardly compare with life on a vineyard.

Abby and Caro were readying their usual meeting at a table they'd set up in her sitting room. They'd started holding their weekly meetings on Fridays and in Sam's room to make it easier on her. She had to smile a few moments later when she saw her mother's gaze sharpen as Will stepped inside the garden wall and entered through the French doors. They never stopped arguing, but at least it was a dialogue. It was certainly better than a drawer full of postcards and two stiff phone calls.

"Stop following me. You wrecked my date with David last night," her mother accused.

Will shrugged. "I'm supposed to be here, Juliana darling. And last night, all I did was happen on you two at the New Dawn Palace."

Juliana slapped the table. "You knew where we were going. You followed me!"

Will sat at the table. "It sounded like a great place to have a good meal. I was as surprised as you that the good doctor asked me to join you." Will's nonchalant gaze sharpened a bit. "He's awfully interested in the finances of the vineyard, isn't he?"

Sam had thought so, too. So had Nic. She fought a sigh and stroked her tummy. They'd agreed on everything. Except love. Nic didn't trust it—or her— anymore. Surprisingly, that hurt the most.

Will's grin drew Sam's attention. Uh-oh. She'd bet Will had brought finances up to see if Doctor Kapp ran with the subject. Apparently, he had.

Her mother crossed her arms. "You're impossible.

Yes, he *was* too interested. There. I admit it. I'm not going to see him again. Don't you dare grin, any of you. Now that Will told him about the amount of the loan, he decided we didn't suit."

Will honestly looked stunned. "I'm sorry, Jule. I didn't mean to see you hurt."

"I'm not hurt. He just beat me to it. I was planning on not seeing him anymore. He was a crushing bore. And Nic thought he was after an interest in the winery. I watched and apparently he was right. David went over the fence as soon as you told him about the loan."

"I am sorry." Will looked and sounded sincere. How did people lie like that and seem so believable? If she'd been able to do that, she'd still have Nic, she thought, and was instantly ashamed. She'd been wrong to manipulate him. And now she was paying for it.

"Don't be sorry," her mother said, sounding sincere and waving off any concern. "I could have disabused him of what you said if I'd wanted to. We no longer have a loan. Nic paid it off. I'm still trying to get him to take a share of the winery."

"He what?" Sam said, sitting up, fighting a full-blown headache now, as well, which only helped to turn up the nausea. "Why would he have done that? When he left, he was worried about finances because his team hadn't been winning enough to cover expenses. When? When did he pay it off?"

"The day he left," Caro said. "We didn't know whether to tell you or not. He wrote that he didn't want you worrying about money. He told us to tell you only if we thought it would upset you less than knowing he'd paid it off."

"He said Harley Bryant looked about to explode," Abby said, grinning. Abby's zoning fights and public criticism of the town's current mayor were becoming legend. "Sammy, Nic obviously cares a great deal for you or he wouldn't have done it," she went on. "You should call him and tell him how difficult a pregnancy you're having."

Sam was afraid he'd think she was trying to manipulate him again. "No. He needs to do what he's doing. Apparently, thanks to me, he needs the money. Besides, if he wanted to be here, he would be. That's final. No calls to Nic about me. Got it?"

Juliana frowned and walked over to the sofa. "Sammy how long have your feet and hands been this swollen?"

Sam looked at her hands. The plain gold band Nic had put on her finger looked two sizes too small. "My feet started swelling about a week ago by the end of the day. Now they just stay swollen. I didn't even realize my hands were involved now." Her mother's concern had alarm shooting through her, making her head hurt worse. "Why? Does it matter?"

"When do you see Doctor Prentice again?" her mother wanted to know.

"Next week, but I was going to call and find out what was safe to take for a headache."

"You have a headache, too? Anything else?" Abby asked.

Sam shrugged. "The nausea came back today," Sam admitted. "I thought I was passed that."

"I think we should call her, Sam," Caro said. "Just to be on the safe side," she added, but she looked worried, too.

Four hours later, Sam was being tucked into bed in her old room so she'd be near the family. Her doctor called what she had preeclampsia. Her headache was caused by high blood pressure. She was on medication for that, but the family had to help monitor it and call the doctor if it went up significantly.

Everyone started on her again to call Nic, but she still refused. The last thing he'd said was that she should try to at least fulfill the second part of their bargain. Once again, Sam faced failure. She'd promised him his shot at immortality. And he needed it. He was risking his life weekly to keep afloat financially and all because he'd paid off their loan. There would be time to call him if she didn't respond to treatment.

Sam shook her head, banishing that thought. The baby's chances of survival were much too slim. The treatment had to work. She had to hang in and last long enough to give her baby a good chance of survival. She couldn't lose the only part of Nic she'd ever have. Besides, she'd promised him this child and she couldn't stand to fail him again.

Not again.

## Chapter Twelve

It was a celebration, Nic reminded himself as he knocked back the rest of his flute of champagne. There was still all kinds of talk among the crews about the near miss he'd had that day. He wished they would get on to another subject. He was trying to forget how close to death he'd come when Freedland lost control of his boat during their final race, cutting across Nic's bow, missing him by inches.

Freedland's wake had sent Nic's boat airborne. After corkscrewing through the air, he'd miraculously landed on the surface right side up and gotten control. It had been too close to what had happened on Long Island Sound. Only Jake's voice coming through his earpiece had called him back and centered him on the race.

With the Freedland boat out of the heat, the battle had been between Nic and the clock as he'd raced to the finish line. He had another Gold Cup to show for it and was one step closer to the World Cup. But since returning to the sport he'd once loved, each victory grew more and more hollow. The World Cup, once his finest moment—his primary goal as each season began—mattered little to him.

Looking around at his team, Nic realized he was in no mood for a party. After tossing a pile of bills on the bar to cover the cost of the impromptu party, he stood to go to his room. His crew protested his desertion but Nic didn't want to dampen their spirits and drag them down with him, so he claimed his shoulder needed icing and left.

He was rarely, if ever, in the mood to celebrate anything anymore. Even signing the contract early that day for the sale of his engine to a world renowned company hadn't lifted Nic's spirits. He wanted to be home, not half a world away.

Hopetown.

Home.

He shook his head. He'd been so angry over Samantha's manipulation that he'd completely missed the truth of the situation until he'd been sitting on a plane with nothing to do but think. By keeping him from knowing about the baby, she'd given him exactly what he'd wanted. More time with her.

He'd won many prizes in his life, but he'd been a prize-winning fool to storm off and leave the only real home he'd ever had. And now that he'd left, he couldn't go back.

Out of habit, Nic stopped at the front desk to check for messages, even though the deal for the engine was signed. He was surprised when the clerk handed him one. It was marked urgent and simply said, "Call home. Zia Juliana."

Alarmed, he hurried to his room and rang the hotel operator. "I need the international operator," he told the man who'd answered, then rattled off the number for Hopewell Manor.

Something had to be gravely wrong. Juliana would not have marked the message urgent otherwise. "I'm ringing your number now," an operator came on the line and said.

*"Grazie,"* he muttered as the phone at the manor rang. Then a man answered. It was not Trey's voice. "This is Niccolò Verdini. Who am I speaking with, please?"

"Nic. It's Will Reiger."

Nic relaxed a bit. Perhaps Zia had come to her senses and was only calling to tell him of her wedding. "You returned. This is good, Will. Samantha had despaired that Zia Juliana would call you."

"She wouldn't have, but Sam's had a rough time. She couldn't handle the work after you left."

Nic's conscience stung. She'd been sick that morning. Of course, she couldn't do the work. "Is she all right now?"

He was sure Will's sigh preceded bad news. "Nic, you'd better get here as fast as you can. Things aren't looking too good for Sam or the baby."

The world dimmed and Nic sank to the bed as his knees gave way. His heart started pounding twice as fast as it had in those critical seconds of the race that day. "What happened?" he managed to ask around the lump in his throat. "What is wrong with my Samantha?"

"Sam has preeclampsia."

"What is it? What is being done to help her?"

"Well, I don't exactly know what it is, but it's something to do with her pregnancy. They'd put her on bed rest in mid-February and had tried treating her at home. She'd gotten worse two weeks ago, and now they've hospitalized her."

"Why did no one tell me of all this before now?"

"Well, first of all, she wouldn't let us. Then when Jule decided to contact you, anyway, you had moved on from Acapulco and we didn't know where to find you. Jamie came up with the idea to set the digital video recorder to your name and it caught your qualifying heat in Qatar yesterday. We called every hotel until we found you."

Nic was furious with himself. "I am so sorry, Will. I never imagined she was having problems."

"No sense beating yourself up now. We found you. That's what's important. She needs you. This is serious, son. The OB wants to take the baby. So far, Sammy's refusing until there's no other choice."

Nic knew she wanted a child, but to risk her life? "Why will she not listen to her doctor?" he wondered aloud as he stood and started pulling his clothes off the rack by the door and tossing them on the bed. Then he pulled down his suitcase. Then Jake, his golden-brown hair still messed from the helmet he'd worn all day, wandered into the room. At the inquisitive narrowing of his blue eyes and his questioning gesture toward the suitcase and clothes, Nic held up his hand telling his friend to wait because Will had begun to answer Nic's rhetorical question.

"She won't listen to any of us, Nic. She keeps saying she's not going to fail you again or her baby. You've got to talk her out of this. We could lose her if you don't."

Nic heard his own voice echoing in his memory, endangering Samantha's life. *Since you broke the first part of our bargain with your silence, I hope you keep the second part.* And then the echo went on to explain why Sam hadn't wanted him told of her difficulties. *I'll let you know where I am so you can let me know of the birth.* He'd as much as told her he didn't want to be involved in the details of her pregnancy or in the baby's birth. Never had he been so ashamed.

"I will make arrangements and get there as quickly as I can, Will. But it will take me at least a day and half of travel after I book my flights. *Grazie* for the call. *Grazie.*"

He hung up and buried his hands in his face, sinking back to the bed. "Samantha and the baby are in trouble. I must leave for home," he told Jake.

"I'll get our travel agent on the line and see what she can do. Should I scratch you for Catalina?"

"I don't think I can come back as part of the racing team, Jake. I will continue to support the team but my heart…it is not in the racing anymore. It is in Pennsylvania," Nic said simply. What he was going to do about that he didn't know. First, he had to get Samantha to save herself.

Nearly twenty-four hours later, Nic got out of the rental car in the parking lot of the Hospital of the University of Pennsylvania, his heart pounding in fear of what he'd find. He'd talked to Zia Juliana as soon as he'd landed at Philadelphia International. She'd assured him there had been no change but that only meant Sam wasn't worse. She wasn't any better, either.

He rushed inside and up to a desk marked. Information. "My wife is here in room 8203. Samantha Verdini," he told the security guard stationed there. He noticed that visiting hours had been over for an hour and went on to explain, "I was away on business when the family called."

"Ah, maternity. Go right on up. Take that elevator to the Silverstein Center on the eighth floor and turn right. Good luck," he said with a smile.

Nic turned away and hurried to the bank of elevators. He supposed the older man thought this was a happy occasion. Indeed, most people assumed medical science had advanced to where pregnancy and delivery were commonplace and no longer as precarious as they had once been. He would never think so again.

He stepped out of the elevator on the eighth floor and followed the signs for the Silverstein Center. He rushed right past a nurses' station intent on finding 8203. "Mr. Verdini?" someone called.

He stopped and turned back to find a tall African-American woman, her white lab coat flapping in the breeze as she rushed around the end of the nurses' station. "Do I know you?" he asked. He didn't think he did.

"My patient, my very stubborn patient, showed me your wedding picture. And your mother-in-law called to say you'd landed and were on your way here." She pursed her lips. "I'm Doctor Prentice, Samantha's OB, and we need to talk."

Nic looked in frustration at the door he'd gotten so close to. "I have been gone for a long time. Can this not wait?"

She smiled. "This won't take long. You need some facts before you see her. I need you to convince Sam to be a little more flexible. I understand her feelings for this child, but she does have a chance to survive now if we take her."

Nic was dead on his feet and right then Samantha's doctor made no sense. "Take her?"

Suspicion entered the doctor's dark gaze. "Deliver her early," she said tentatively. "Your child is a girl, Mr. Verdini. I assumed you knew."

Every soft emotion he'd ever felt washed over Nic. A girl. He would have a daughter. Samantha's daughter. He was in the middle of picturing a little blond-haired girl with brown eyes, when reality crashed back into his world as the doctor went on.

"You *are* on good terms with Samantha, aren't you?"

"I love my wife," Nic said simply. To him it was all that mattered.

"Good. What you need to know going in is that the

baby's chances are pretty good now. Not as good as if Sam had made it all the way, but she's close to thirty-two weeks now. If she goes into full eclampsia, danger to both of them increases. Then there would be no choice. We'd have to take the baby, or they both won't make it. I'd rather it not be with my patient on death's door."

It still seemed unreal that Samantha could die. She was so alive! "What would happen to her...to Samantha...if it becomes this eclampsia?"

"Her kidneys could fail. It could cause liver damage or brain hemorrhage. She could go into convulsions. Your wife is walking a fine line between preeclampsia and eclampsia right this minute."

"If this child, our little girl—" Nic's eyes blurred and his throat closed as the magnitude of the question he needed to ask hit him. He cleared his throat. He didn't know how he was going to say the words, but he knew now that he needed all the information he could get before seeing Samantha. "If Samantha agrees and you are wrong...and the baby does not live...can my wife still have other children?"

Doctor Prentice closed her eyes and sighed. "I hate when a patient and their family members ask me questions like that. The truth is, I can't promise anything. I wish I could but there's no telling. I will say there's a strong indication that another pregnancy would be possible because of her ease of getting pregnant this time. And preeclampsia is rarely a problem in second pregnancies. Now, are you going to help me convince her?"

He took a deep breath. "I am," Nic said, and turned

away, praying he could do as promised. Quietly, he pushed the door open and stepped inside. Samantha seemed to be asleep. The room was dim, but he could still see her. And, when he stepped closer to the bed, he grew more alarmed. She didn't look like herself. Her features were blunted, her face swollen. Not as swollen as her hands, though. The wedding ring that had been just a bit loose when he'd put it on her finger would have to be cut off to be removed.

He looked again at her face and she opened her eyes; joy flared in their hazel depths. It lightened his heart that she would be so glad to see him. But then, as she became aware of her surroundings, her joy turned to panic and then stubbornness. She turned her face away. "I told them not to call you."

Nic walked around the bed so that he could see her face. "Don't be angry with them. I should be here. I should have been here all along."

She looked up at him then. "That wasn't part of the bargain," she reminded him coolly. In her gaze was a mixture of pain and anger.

And her words pierced his heart. He deserved her anger but she didn't deserve the pain. Had she felt this agony every time he'd reminded her he would leave once she'd conceived? Of course she had. She had told him she loved him and he'd wounded her this way on a daily basis week after week. No wonder she'd kept the truth from him.

Sam watched as Nic sank into the chair facing the bed. She wanted to turn away but she'd craved the sight of his face for so long. "Samantha, I never meant to hurt you and I have come to understand that you didn't mean to hurt me."

Of all the things she had expected to hear, that was not one of them. "I didn't mean to, Nic, but I did. I was desperate and I guess desperation makes people do things they'd never do otherwise. It was bad enough that you were determined to leave, but you were going back to racing. Every time I closed my eyes, I saw your accident." She couldn't keep the tears damming in her throat from entering her voice. "I saw them pulling you onto that rescue chopper. Limp and…" Her voice broke. "I had to stop you."

His fingers rose to seal her lips. "Shh, shh, *cara*. You must not upset yourself this way." As if needing to touch her again, he swept a few stray locks of hair off her face. "Now, tell me why you have been so stubborn with your doctor. You should not risk your life this way. Will says you are doing this to fulfill your promise to me. I never meant to imply that you would be foolish during your pregnancy and endanger our child. I meant only that you were to keep the promise to tell me of the birth. *Cara*, I don't want this child at the cost of your life."

Sam huffed out a breath. "I think I knew that, but don't you see, I'm doing it again? I love our baby and I love you and I'm failing both of you."

"Samantha—"

"No. Listen. I'm not being as reckless as they all

seem to think. I want her to have the best chance she can have. Trey recommended a top neonatal doctor. That's why I'm here at the Hospital of the University of Pennsylvania. Children's Hospital is affiliated with this hospital and has some of the best neonatologists in the world. Trey's friend is on staff and he ordered tests.

"At first, she wasn't viable. Her lungs were too immature, but she's come a long way. I only have to hold on for three more days. The difference gained for her between twenty-nine weeks and thirty-two weeks is incredible. We're almost there. It's Friday now. By Monday, she'll have grown over an inch just this week and she'll have put on nearly a pound." She caressed her tummy, imagining her child could feel her touch. "She's learning to breathe right now. That's big, Nic." She rolled over and pulled the picture of the baby from her drawer. It was from the three-dimensional ultrasound she'd had just last week.

"This is who we're talking about. Look at her sweet little face."

Nic took the snapshot and stared at it. When he looked up, tears spilled from his eyes. "She is perfect. So perfect."

She grabbed his hand, desperately needing another ally. "Thirty-two weeks means so much more than that. She's growing eyelashes and eyebrows. There's a substance being produced right now called surfactant that they need for healthy lungs. They can usually feed normally by the end of the thirty-second week, too. She'll have less chance of learning problems and depression in her later life. I'm fighting for the quality of her whole life here. Three more days. That's all I'm after. If I get worse, we'll have to do the C-section because then she'd be in trouble, too."

"But what of you? The doctor said—"

Sam sighed and Nic stopped. "I know all about the risks. I'm not foolishly playing with our lives. I promise. I'm about twenty feet from the delivery room! If I get worse, they can whisk me in there and do their thing. I promise."

Nic looked confused and uncertain. "I promised everyone I'd talk you into ending this." He looked down at the ultrasound snapshot, then put his hand on her tummy. "I have never felt more torn. I see your goal and it is admirable, but the risk…" He shook his head. "I cannot think of a world without you in it. But this is ultimately your decision. Your life that is in danger. I have no right to pressure you. But neither will I leave your side again. Sleep, *piccola*."

"Little one?" Sam laughed, and caressed her tummy, covering his hand. Was this man blind? She didn't even know herself in the mirror anymore. "I'm a long way from little, these days."

"Sleep," he ordered with mock severity, and reached for her other hand as he scooted the padded rocking chair closer. His arm and the hand holding hers rested on the mattress alongside her. "You sleep. I sleep. This is a very comfortable chair."

She turned her head and looked at him through

the top bars of the bed. "You should go home," she protested.

"No," he declared, shaking his head and looking vulnerable and stubborn at once.

"There are rules about this. They'll come in and make you leave."

"No, they won't. I will not leave your side until our child is delivered and you are healthy again. That is final. Now, rest." He propped his feet on the smaller guest chair. Tilting the rocker back, he closed his eyes.

She'd forgotten how stubborn he could be. Luckily, she was just as stubborn as he was—maybe more. Sam sighed. Sleep was a long way off.

Though she was relieved and happy to have her friend back, she couldn't help but notice that he'd never said he loved her. And, though he was there, he hadn't said anything about not returning to racing as soon as she'd had the baby. She wondered what he'd think of the name she'd chosen for their daughter.

It only seemed fair to name the baby for Nic. Without him and his offer, she wouldn't have had this opportunity to feel her child growing beneath her heart. She'd never have known the thrill of that first flutter, that first kick. She'd never have spent a night last week awake and worrying about the strange rhythmic, convulsive movements she'd felt coming from her child. She'd never have felt the elation she did when Doctor Wolf, Trey's neonatologist friend, allayed her fears, explaining that her baby had hiccups and that hiccups were a good sign. It proved that Nicole had definitely been in her thirtieth week.

Her door opened then and Doctor Prentice stuck her head in, no doubt hoping for a change in the status quo. Sam simply smirked and waved, enjoying her victory. Nic was at her side and on her side.

She just wished he loved her, too.

## Chapter Thirteen

*N*ic fought the bucking wheel, knowing he had to keep the boat under control or die. And he couldn't die. He had a wife and child to care for. The engine cut out and the boat slowed, but the bucking and shuddering only increased. A sound reached his ears, then. It sounded like a human choking, not an engine.

Nic bolted upright in the chair. He was awake, but his heart still pounded as if he were still trapped in the dream. It had been so real. Then he felt vibrations from his dream against his shoulder, so he twisted toward the bed only to discover that the vibrations came from Samantha. Her eyes were open but had rolled back. Her body shook and bucked. Her spine was bowed backward in an arch. He catapulted to his feet, rounded the bed and yanked open the door to the hall.

"My wife," he shouted, running toward the nurses' station. "Someone help."

His call was apparently unnecessary. Three nurses were already running toward the room. He jogged back and found himself pushed to the side by a tall male nurse. Nic watched in fear as they went to work. A blond nurse gave Samantha an injection that calmed the shuddering and eased her breathing. Another nurse entered and said she'd called for Doctor Prentice. Then they unlocked the wheels of the bed and pushed her across the hall to the delivery room. Samantha hadn't gotten her three days. He looked at the clock. In fact, she barely gotten three hours.

He wanted to follow, but there were papers for him to sign. Papers to authorize an anesthetist. To authorize a cesarean section. To agree with the use of a respirator on the baby. And for the same help for Samantha if she needed it. He had no choice but to trust the doctor's integrity because there was no way to read them all and not hold up the surgery. So he signed, and prayed and called the manor. Zia Juliana tried to be brave but was clearly as terrified as he was. The family was on the way.

Numb with fear, he stood in Samantha's empty room and looked around. Plastic tubing, monitor wires, paper and plastic wrappers from God only knew what items they'd been using lay on every surface where they had been tossed. The room was a disaster.

Just like his life.

Then someone came into the room and he pivoted.

The same male nurse who'd explained the paperwork stood there holding a set of scrubs. "Doc says you can be there. Put these on and hurry or you'll miss the birth. When we go in you can stand near your wife's head. She isn't conscious, though, just so you know."

"Why would she be unconscious?"

The nurse hesitated. "There can be a lot of reasons but taking the baby will more than likely reverse all her symptoms. Doc Prentice is the best. Try to relax, but hurry."

Nic found he had no voice so he nodded and took the clothes. Hands shaking, he stripped and donned the green scrubs, a mask, covers for his shoes. He hadn't thought they'd let him in the room, but he wasn't about to voice his doubts for fear the nurse would realize this was a mistake.

Before Nic knew it, the same man returned and ushered him in to stand near Samantha. Luckily, they had a drape in place so he couldn't actually see the surgical site. Thank God. He didn't think he could take that. He just focused on Samantha's face. He nearly missed seeing his tiny daughter's first moments because he couldn't look away from her mother. But Doctor Prentice called his name and held up the baby for him to see. And only then, when he saw how tiny and fragile the baby was, did he fully understand Samantha's fight to hold off this moment as long as possible.

Doctor Wolf, the neonatologist Trey had recommended, rushed in just as their daughter arrived in the world. He scooped the baby out of Doctor Prentice's upraised hands and immediately wrapped her in a blanket he'd brought into the room with him. Wolf was a not a big man, but the baby looked so minuscule in his hands that Nic's fear grew. And he hadn't thought he could be more terrified than he'd been.

Nic was suddenly aware of the silence in the room. The baby wasn't crying. Before Nic could ask why, Wolf and the baby were gone. He'd whisked her off to somewhere called the ICN, the male nurse explained. The same nurse, who Nic now supposed must have been assigned to watch him, went on to explain that ICN stood for Intensive Care Nursery.

Paralyzed, he stood, his mind reeling from fear and wonder. Never before had he been so torn. He wanted to follow the baby. To protect her. To comfort her in case she was afraid. She'd been rudely pulled from Samantha's body and handed over to a stranger. He was her father and he'd barely gotten a chance to see her before they took her away. But he needed to stay with Samantha, as well.

Doctor Prentice obviously saw his dilemma. "Go to the ICN. You can't do anything here for your wife. That's my job. We'll get her stabilized. I promise to send for you if there's any change."

"I promised I would stay at her side," he explained. "I want to be with her, but…" He glanced toward the door they'd taken the baby through.

"The ICN is just through that door, then across the hall. Nicole may need to hear her daddy's voice once they get her stable."

Nicole? Nic felt as if he'd taken a punch to his solar plexus. Samantha had planned to name their child for him? Doctor Prentice must have seen his shook. "That's right, handsome. She plans to name the baby after you."

He nodded, too overcome to speak and moved away after one last look at Samantha. As the door to the hall closed behind him, he heard one of the delivery nurses say, "If he loves her so much, why the hell wasn't he around till now?"

As he walked across the hall, Nic wondered how much guilt one man could handle. Since learning Samantha was in danger, he'd declared his love for her to his friend Jake, to her doctor, to Will, to Zia Juliana when they'd spoken after his plane landed. However, he had not told his wife.

Because he couldn't.

She loved him. She'd said it the day he'd left and he believed her. But to tell her of his love would have given her false hope that he would stay after the birth of the baby. He hadn't thought staying—building a life with Sam and their child—was possible, not if he was to keep the child safe from his own negative influences.

Now, though, after seeing her tiny form arrive unprotected into a alien world, Nic knew he'd been wrong. He would never do anything to hurt her. He would give his life to protect hers. He wanted only what was best for her.

He stepped inside the ICN. It was so quiet he could hear his own breathing. The staff seemed to go out of their way to keep the room as quiet as possible. And he was glad because he knew a moment of tremendous relief when he picked up on the little mewing sounds his tiny daughter made. She was breathing. She was still alive.

Nic lost track of time, staring at the sweet scrap of humanity Samantha had given life. The staff in the ICN worked with efficiency and care, washing her, measuring and weighing her. Listening to her heart. When they did a blood test, Nicole made her displeasure known with a loud cry.

Startled by the discordant sound, Nic stared at his daughter, shocked that so loud a sound could come from one so small.

Apparently, the neonatologist was pleased. He chuckled, and said, "Now, that's what we like to hear. Strong healthy lungs. Well, little one, your mommy did a good job for you. Mr. Verdini, I think we have a full thirty-two weeker here. She may even be a few days beyond. My guess is that Samantha must have conceived early in her cycle. She gave your child a heck of a good chance. She's over two thousand grams. I'll save you the math, that's four pounds, eight ounces. Let's get you over here to hold her and do a little bonding. You can be the hero who saved her from all of us meanies. Right, sweetheart?" he cooed to the wailing baby.

Nic looked around. Was the doctor talking to him? "Me? I can hold her?" Nic asked, hearing the awe in his own voice.

"Come on. Settle yourself in that rocker in the corner. You hold on to her while I write the particulars in her chart. Relax, Pop, she won't break," Wolf urged. "We have her on a little oxygen to help pink her up so don't let it alarm you. It looks like her lungs are doing just fine. She just needs a little boost for a few weeks or so."

Nic didn't need a second invitation. He did as ordered and accepted his daughter from Wolf. *"Grazie,"* he said, but his throat was too choked with emotion to say more. She was light as a feather, he thought as he cradled her in his arms, staring down at perfection. And tumbled into love for the second time in less than a year.

They'd wrapped her in a pink blanket and had a little pink ski cap on her head. She had a hint of the fine little eyelashes and eyebrows Samantha had mentioned. *"Bambina di papà,"* he whispered.

"So our little one's going to be bilingual," an African-American nurse hovering over his shoulder commented. "What did you tell her?"

Nic smiled up at her. "Much like a wonderful old song I heard played at the wedding of a friend, 'Daddy's Little Girl.'"

Misty-eyed, Nic looked back down at Nicole. At her tiny nose. Her stubborn little chin. "Look at you, sweet one. You look just like your mama." He sniffled.

"Hold her against your chest," the sweet-faced nurse watching them said. "She's going to have a little trouble staying warm for a while because she didn't get time to put on a good layer of fat. She'll spend most of her time in an incubator. It'll be temperature controlled to help her keep warm."

"I have many questions but…" He glanced through the wide windows of the ICN toward the delivery room, so terrified for Samantha his fear overshadowed his joy, turning it bittersweet. "Samantha. I— What if she never sees our child?"

What if he never had the chance to tell her he loved her? That he wanted them to be a family? As if conjured by the word, a tap on the hall glass drew both his attention and the doctor's. Nic was never so glad to see someone as he was to see his *padrina*, Zia Juliana. Since his accident, whenever he needed someone, her family had been there. He wanted to be a permanent part of their little circle of love.

Doctor Wolf apparently heard him express his continued worry for Samantha because he said, "Suppose I go find out how Mama is doing while you bond with your little one? We'll hand them all a mask and gowns so you can show her off to her grandmom and aunts and uncles."

Those moments introducing his precious daughter to the rest of her family were the first not spent in torment for two long days. Just after Caroline and Trey arrived, Doctor Wolf had returned with upsetting news. Though a CAT scan had shown no brain damage, Samantha remained unconscious, her blood pressure still dangerously high.

Zia Juliana and Abby stayed with him through the small hours of the morning, but there were guests at Cliff Walk so Abby needed to return home. Zia had admonished him to get some sleep, but sleep felt far away. He sat next to Samantha's bed with all of the dire warnings from Dr. Prentice echoing in his mind. After a while, all the bleeps and beeps of various monitors formed an almost musical background for desperate prayers to a creator he'd long ignored. Finally, the cacophony of the machines lulled Nic into a restless sleep.

Sam swam to the surface of the tumbling murky river. Dizzily she burst into the sunshine and forced her eyes open. But it wasn't a canopy of trees she saw above her but a plain white ceiling. The hospital's ceiling.

Then she remembered. She was in the hospital trying to save her child. She became aware of a sharp cutting pain and moved her hand to rub her tummy and encountered a thick bandage. It took only a millisecond for panic to set in. The baby was gone! They'd taken the baby!

"My baby! Where's my baby?" she shouted.

Nic suddenly filled her vision and sat next to her on the bed, caressing her arms. "Shh, shh, *mia preziosa*, Nicole is wonderful. Perfect. Doing marvelously well."

Sam focused on Nic, who'd apparently still been sitting next to her exactly where he'd been when she fell asleep. But that made no sense. They'd taken the baby. He had to have let them.

"You lied," she accused. "You told me you understood. How could you go behind my back and let them take her?"

Nic gripped her by her shoulder in a firm but gentle grasp. "No. No. No. I would never betray you that way. Your trust is everything to me. You had begun having convulsions as I'd sat with you the night I'd arrived."

Sam frowned. She didn't remember, but she did feel much weaker than usual. "I went into eclampsia?"

Nic nodded and pushed a lock of hair off her cheek. "It's clear you don't remember. I confess I am glad of that. You have been so ill. So dangerously ill. It is two days since she was born."

Hope blossomed in Sam's chest. Two days, and her child was still alive. And Nic said she was doing well. "When can I see her?"

"As soon as your doctor says you can go to the Intensive Care Nursery."

"Intensive Care Nursery? She's really okay?"

Nic pulled an indignant face. "Okay? My daughter is more than *okay*. She is the most beautiful baby in the ICN. In the whole hospital. Perhaps the world."

She found the strength to chuckle at his foolishness. "Somebody's smitten."

"No. I am fully in love. A tiny child holds my heart in the palm of her little hand."

Hungry for any news of Nicole, Sam very nearly begged, "What else can you tell me about her?"

Nic was glad to oblige. He sat back a bit, which was good since he tended to talk with his hands constantly in motion when he was excited. He cocked his knee up on the bed some more and leaned forward. He reminded her of Jamie on Christmas morning. Eyes alive and bright with excitement and his enthusiasm pouring out for all to see.

"Let me see," he began. "She is quite indignant when they prick her foot for blood tests. What a pair of lungs she has when she shows her displeasure. Doctor Wolf feels she was delivered at thirty-two weeks plus a day or so. He says you must have conceived earlier in your cycle than normal, which could explain why you didn't conceive in Vegas. Oh, and she was four pounds, eight ounces at birth. She is such a wonderful eater that she has lost little of her birth weight. I feed her often but not every time because she has stolen the hearts of everyone in the ICN."

Even knowing her baby was doing well, Sam was still left feeling empty. As if part of her was missing. Her heart ached. Her empty arms ached to cuddle her child. Her Nicole. She just couldn't wait anymore. "I need to see her. To hold her."

"And you will. I will let the nurses know you have awakened in a short while but first we need to talk. Please, can you wait?"

Wondering what could be so important and terrified he'd say he was leaving, she cautiously agreed.

"I wish to apologize for what I did to you while I was back on the circuit. I will never do that again. I promise you."

Sam didn't know what to make of that. "I don't understand."

He groaned. "I am sure you don't. Once again I am doing a poor job of saying what is in my heart."

She hated that her difficult pregnancy had heaped such guilt on Nic's shoulders. He'd only been trying to help her with this bargain marriage of theirs. He'd offered to give her the baby that was her heart's desire; he certainly didn't ask her to love him. It wasn't his fault that along the way he'd become part of her dream. "Nic, you were free to leave. That was part of the bargain."

A sound of pure frustration filled the room. Then he

spat out a sharp curse in Italian. "If you bring up that bargain again, Samantha," he said, "I swear to you, I will scream."

She let out an unladylike snorted. "You sort of already did."

He huffed out a breath and nodded. "I cannot apologize for that." He took her hand. "You see, I love you. Is that plain enough for you to understand? And so, about our...bargain," he said through gritted teeth, sounding supremely annoyed by the word even when he said it. "I wish to renegotiate."

Sam wondered if her mind was clear enough for this serious a talk. "Wait a minute. Do you love me like a friend, a lover or a wife?"

He sighed. "I am greatly in love with you in all those ways and more."

She couldn't fight the smile she knew had bloomed on her lips. "You are?"

He nodded and kissed the hand he held. "This is the reason for the renegotiation. I will not go back to racing."

Relieved, she nearly sighed. She didn't think she could handle it again if he went off to climb into the cockpit of one of those death machines. It sounded as if he might be about to hand her everything she'd dreamed of, but how could he give up something he loved as much as he loved racing. He'd given up his relationship with his father over it. "You're sure?"

"Since my accident I have been less sure I want to race, though I still love the sport. But only since I received word that you were ill have I understood what it is like to stand back and watch someone you care for risk their life."

"What do you want to do?"

He didn't hesitate but sounded uncertain. "I want to live with you. Raise Nicole with you. Grow old with you. Do you think you would want those things with me? I know my reputation with women makes me look as if I am a poor candidate for marriage—long-term marriage—but I will never betray you. I notice other women now only to compare them to you. And none of them ever measure up. You are one of a kind and I want you to be mine."

Would she want... To hear this man—this lady-killer international playboy—sound so unsure because he wanted a life with her humbled Sam. Tears welled up in her eyes and she opened her mouth to tell him nothing would make her happier, but she could only nod. Then a question occurred to her. She cleared her throat—Nic was already wiping her eyes and muttering about always making her cry. She finally managed to ask, "Why did you stay away if you weren't angry anymore?"

He scrubbed a hand over his face, his stubbled chin. Then he raked his wavy hair with his hand before expelling the breath he'd been holding. "My initial anger was habit. You'd held the truth from me to manipulate me. So I left in a huff. But I was scarcely in the air when I realized that by keeping your pregnancy from me you had given me what I most wanted—more time with you."

"Then, why didn't you just come back?"

Nic shook his head, his lips pursed in annoyance. "I

couldn't. It was that damn bargain again. You were pregnant so there was no reason for me to remain with you. I still didn't think I could be in your life because that would expose Nicole to my poor parenting."

Sam had heard that one time too many. If he didn't want to hear about the bargain, then she didn't want to hear him spouting that claptrap! "For heaven's sake, we all have the free will to become the people we want to be. Children aren't carbon copies of their parents."

"I know that. Now. I knew the moment I saw Nicole that I would lay down my life for her before I would ever do or say something to harm her." He shook his head, his gaze bleak as if even revisiting those times was painful. "I didn't believe this kind of protective love existed. It made me rethink my father and my feelings as you were risking your life. I called him. I don't think we will ever be the close family you were blessed with, but we have peace between us now. He congratulates us on our child and promises to come see her."

"I'm glad for you, Nic. And for Nicole. I'd like her to get to know all of her family."

Nic grimaced. "All did not go well with the call. There was a family dinner that night because Nonna was there. So was Gina and her family. She shouted something vile and stormed out of the room when she heard my father promise to come see us. I confess I am not surprised, but I had hoped there would be a change in her. Her jealousy goes too deep for us to be on friendly terms, it seems."

She held her hand out to him and he took it again.

"I'm sorry, Nic. You can borrow Abby and Caro anytime you need a sister, but I warn you they can be a pain in the neck, too, sometimes. I think that's part of the job description."

"Mine is a pain much farther south," he said, with a deadpan look that made her chuckle. "My sister does not know what a wonderful sister-in-law she has given up with her stubbornness. I only wonder what she will do to try to cause trouble this time."

"Do you really think she'll do something?"

"I learned a long time ago not to think anything was too much for her to do. And she did threaten. Remember the chess reference in her message when we returned from Las Vegas?" Nic shrugged and went on as if he was used to having his sister be a shadow in his life. "I did talk to Nonna and told her how well Nicole is doing now. She was very pleased at her progress. I think she might have gone to see my father to tell him of Nicole's birth. She promised to go to Mass all month to pray for her."

"That was sweet."

Nic rolled his eyes. "And to pray for us. Nonna can be very sweet but she can also be a tyrant. I hope you don't mind, but I also confessed the truth of our marriage."

Now that surprised her. "Was that wise?"

"I did not want a lie present in our lives, *cara*. I also told her I wished ours to be a real marriage but that I was unsure how you felt about it and me."

Sam reached up and ran the back of her hand over his jaw. "But I told you how I felt before you left."

Guilt shadowed Nic's eyes again. He took her hand and

kissed the back of her fingers. "You did and then I rushed off in a huff and abandoned you to fight for our daughter's life alone. I was unsure how you would feel now."

"Love doesn't die that easily, Nic."

He nodded. "Nonna being Nonna told me our marriage is real no matter how it began. She also said that even though I am an idiot for weaving so tangled a web, you are too smart to let a prime catch like me get away." He grinned playfully and tilted his head. "She is right as usual, no?"

Sam smiled. "She is right as usual, yes."

Nic gently kissed the hand he held. "I have kept you from our daughter too long. I should report you are awake. Perhaps they will let you see her tonight."

Sam watched Nic round the bed, throw her a playful kiss and duck into the hall. Two questions popped into her head at nearly the same moment. How had she gotten so lucky? And why was Nic so sure his sister would still try to cause trouble? Remembering Gina's wedding message to Nic, Sam dismissed the threat.

Nicole's birth and their mutual love had been check and mate. Theirs was no bargain marriage, anymore. Of course there was nothing Gina could do.

## Chapter Fourteen

Later that evening, Nic opened the door to Samantha's hospital room. He hated to disturb her but he had no choice. The cosmos seemed to be out to separate them. The door squeaked and Sam turned her head. "Nic? What on earth are you doing here at this time of the night. Tell me you didn't come all the way back here to feed Nikki."

He grinned. "She already has a nickname? She is Nikki? But no one will know if she is a boy or girl." He chuckled and shook his head. "No, that isn't true. Even if she is a tomboy like her mother, she will be as beautiful as her mother, too. I will have a Sammy and a Nikki and be fighting the men and boys off with a stick." He frowned. "But what happens when we have a son?

Will we call him Sue like that very funny country-and-western song?"

She laughed as he meant her to. "You are a nutcase. So why are you here at this hour?"

He'd meant her to laugh, but the situation was no laughing matter. "Samantha, Jake Forester has been badly hurt in Catalina. Jake has no family but an elderly mother who cannot travel. I must go to California. I promise I will stay only as long as is necessary. I don't want to leave, but he has come to be a good friend in these last weeks and his condition is serious. I promise to stay no longer than necessary."

"When I think of how alone you must have been in that hospital on Long Island... Of course you should go. Nikki and I are both doing great. I'm just sorry about Jake."

So was Nic but that didn't make leaving any easier. Nor did it lessen his panic when a tabloid reporter tracked him down three days later as he left the hospital in Anaheim to which Jake had been airlifted.

The reporter wanted his comment on an article in another rag about him and Monique Dubois, the woman who'd been his lover when he'd been hurt in Long Island. Nic usually didn't give tabloid reporters the time of day but something made him take the clipping and read it.

The article stated that Monique had confessed to the author of the article that she felt overwhelmed by guilt because she and Nic had picked up their affair where they'd left off when he'd returned to the circuit. She now feared their involvement had caused the problems in Samantha's pregnancy.

Nic stared at the reporter, who took a step back. "Look, I didn't write it. I'm just here to give you a chance to comment."

"You want my comment? It would be unprintable. But here. Print this. I have not seen Monique Dubois since she lifted a thousand dollars from my wallet while I was in surgery in Long Island, New York, last June. I love my wife. I would not dishonor her this way. Her illness was a common complication of first pregnancies that could have meant her death and our child's, as well. This is not something that should be used as fodder for your brand of journalism. But I will say that both my wife and my daughter are doing well now. Our marriage is strong and I am going to be too boring to waste your time on after this. There. You have your comment."

Nic's temper flared when the reported looked disappointed. "Do you wish a more sensational story? Perhaps you could write about how I took your camera and beat you over the head with it. Go away or I will happily cooperate with a more interesting version of our meeting."

The reporter wisely rushed away and Nic hurriedly crossed the street to the hotel where he'd been staying. He placed a call to the manor. No one was there, which was quite odd. Nor did Abby answer at Cliff Walk. He tried the winery and again there was no answer. Then he remembered Samantha was supposed to go home that day. He tried her hospital room but she didn't answer, either. Where was everyone? He called the only two family cell-phone numbers he knew. Abby's, then

Juliana's. Neither seemed to be turned on, but at least he could leave messages. After he hung up, he realized he must have sounded desperate as he denied the lies in the article and asked them to relay his message to Samantha. He even tried to reach Samantha's doctor, worried for her health. He could only reach Doctor Prentice's answering service. They told him the doctor was camped out at the hospital and abruptly disconnected the call.

Nic returned to the Anaheim hospital where Jake was now out of intensive care. A copy of the same troubling clipping sat on the tray in front of his friend.

"A little worm of a reporter was in here," Jake told him. "He got past the nurses by telling them he was a team member."

"I should have hit him with his camera as I'd offered."

Jake snorted. "I sent him packing after telling him you may as well become a monk considering all the action you've seen since you hit the circuit again. Oh, and I hope you don't mind, I said you'd spent weeks mooning because you'd missed your wife and that I should know what you'd been up to because I'd shared a room with you. Now go home. The doctors all say I'm out of the woods." He'd grinned and added that he'd get better much faster without Nic hovering and pacing.

Nic was at the airport in Anaheim within the hour. The first thing he did was stop at the newsstand and grab a copy of the *Tattler*. That turned his panic up a notch.

It had been on the stands for nearly a week, so he was sure Sam must have heard about it.

When he reached the ticket counter he hit a roadblock he swore to get around. It was the reason he'd been unable to reach anyone in Pennsylvania. Every major city from Chicago east was crippled by a massive storm system that had spread a thick layer of ice and wet snow over everything. Power lines were down, communication and most public transportation had been knocked out almost everywhere.

As Nic watched the monitors, one flight east after another popped up as cancelled. Airports all across the northeast corridor were shutting down. What was it with Samantha and bad weather? Nic swore Mother Nature was out to get them both.

Sam slowly made her way to the nursery to feed Nikki. She was sure some time with her baby would calm her down. She was supposed to have left that morning but, when her blood pressure went up early in the day, Doctor Prentice refused to discharge her. It had gone up because Sam had gotten upset over an article in a tabloid another patient left lying in the conservatory. About the same time Sam was reading the article, a heavy snow had begun to fall and within an hour—an hour she'd spent with medical personnel poking her, prodding her and tracking her blood pressure—she'd somehow missed Nic at his hotel. Between the delay and the snow she'd been unable to locate him since.

Normally, she wouldn't give the article a second thought. The problem was that, when she woke after having the baby, Nic had very nearly confirmed what the article said. He'd apologized for what he'd done to her while back on the circuit. It had confused her then and she'd asked him what he meant. He hadn't really answered. Instead, he'd said something about having trouble expressing himself and had gone on to talk about understanding her worry with his racing because of the danger she'd been in.

She didn't want to believe the article, but there was a picture with it. And Sam had lied to Nic about the baby. He'd been so angry. She'd never seen him angry before that. When he'd left, there'd been no real commitment between them. Nic had been free to do as he pleased according to their bargain. Still, she'd be terribly hurt if he'd turned to someone else after making love to her.

Sam was determined not to form an opinion about what the article said until she could ask Nic straight out. There was no way she would believe a tabloid over him if he denied it. And she would work very hard to forgive him if he admitted it. Unfortunately, he'd checked out of his hotel and she couldn't get through to his cell phone.

She reached the nursery, determined to put problems aside and enjoy her child. After a wonderful hour feeding Nikki, helping bathe her and change her, Sam strolled back to her room feeling much better. Nic loved her. She was sure of it.

When Sam entered her room, she found there were two strangers lying in wait—one a short greasy man holding a video camera, the other a tall blond woman in a skirt that was much too short and heels, so high, she looked in danger of toppling onto her face.

"What are you doing in here? No one is allowed on the maternity ward at this time of the day," she told them, and noticed that man had hoisted the camera to sit upon his shoulder.

"I had to see you," the blond woman said after a quick glance at the camera.

Sam recognized her. She was the woman who'd given the interview for the article that had tied Sam's stomach in knots.

"I had to see you to tell you I'm sorry," the living Barbie doll said, and advanced across the room so that the camera was now trained on both of them. "It was kismet when Niccolò and I ran into each other in the hotel lobby in Portimao," she went on. "I tried to resist, but he just swept me off my feet. Literally. How can a girl resist a man who carries her off an elevator all the way to his room and tosses her onto his bed? It was like coming home to be in his arms again." She frowned a little. "He lied to me, too, you know. He said your marriage was a sham. I can't tell you how shocked I was at first to hear he flew back here to be with you. But then I realized Niccolò is like that."

Sam eyed the tall blonde. The woman had six inches on Sam—and six years. Thanks to the new body image she'd gained by seeing herself through Nic's eyes, Sam could see that Monique probably outweighed her by a good twenty pounds. The model also looked heavier than she had in the picture of her and Nic that had accompanied the article.

It was an old picture.

Tears misted Sam's eyes. She wouldn't have to ask Nic a thing. The whole thing was a lie. "Are you saying Nic picked you up and carried you off an elevator, down a hall, into a hotel room and all the way to the bed? And then he *tossed* you onto the bed?"

Now Monique looked unsure but she realized what she'd said was on camera. "Well, yes. He did. It was very romantic and so macho."

Sam remembered Nic carrying her. It *had* been terribly romantic. She also knew it had hurt him. "I don't know what you thought you'd get out of this."

How could they try to hurt Nic like this? She turned away from them, fighting tears. It was so unfair. And all to sell a few papers. She couldn't spend one more second in a room with these awful people. Her hormones had her emotions bouncing all over the place. She walked to the door and opened it. "Get out! You aren't allowed in here and I don't need this kind of upset. Leave us alone."

The reporter having failed to get a catfight on tape didn't move, though Monique scurried out. "What about the fact that your marriage isn't a real one? That it was a deal you two made to get Verdini the rest of the money from his grandfather's will?" the reporter asked.

That knocked Sam even more off center. How would he know that? Nic would never have told anyone about that. And when had Nic gone from the press's darling to someone with a bull's-eye painted on his chest?

"No comment?" he goaded.

Sam raised her chin. She was not letting this oily little man and his camera destroy everything she and Nic had built between them. "Nic's grandfather's will didn't say a thing about having children. It doesn't get much more real than diapers and middle-of-the-night feedings. Nic took nearly every nighttime feeding until Jake Forester crashed in Catalina." Remembering seeing Nic hold their tiny daughter before he left, she teared up even more. "I don't know who told you our marriage isn't real, but that's my answer. Now, get out or I'll call security!"

He finally turned off his camera and left. Sam sank into the rocker next to her bed wiping away her tears. She looked at her damp fingers. How the hell had her life turned itself upside down like this? And now they had her crying on film!

Some kind of reaction to all the excitement set in then. Sam realized she was shaking and her head was pounding again. She pressed her call button and crawled into bed, feeling insubstantial and agitated. When a nurse came in to check, Sam's blood pressure had shot up again.

Sam had slept for a few hours when the howling wind woke her. She'd forgotten the ice storm. Maybe Nic had tried to call. Or maybe he was as in the dark about the article as she had been. She decided to try one more time to reach him, but this time she called Jake Forester's hospital, thinking maybe Nic was with him.

Sam was surprised when she was connected to Jake and not an ICU nurse.

"Samantha. Was Nic ever able to get through to you?" he asked immediately.

"No, I'd hoped he was there with you."

"I sent him home. The boy's a basket case about an article some rag printed about him. You'd think he'd know to ignore that claptrap by now," he drawled, his Tennessee accent evident. "I heard what a mess a whole half of the eastern seaboard is. I'm sure Nic didn't know about it, but he was desperate to get there. I'd bet you'll see him as soon as he can plow through the storm out there."

As night fell, Sam stood at her window looking out at the city beyond her window. It looked a bit like a mad baker had gone wild. The buildings were glazed with ice and frosted beneath it with a heavy wet snow that had stuck to everything, even the windward facades of the historic University of Pennsylvania buildings. Nothing moved as the freezing rain-and-snow mix continued to fall.

After feeding Nikki again at ten, she returned to her room in time to flip on the eleven o'clock news. Thousands were without phones and electricity, which explained why she'd been unable to get a call through to the manor. They reported that the airport had been closed since the early afternoon but was due to open within an hour or two. The major arteries leading into center city Philadelphia where the hospital was were being salted again and were passable, but were still slick and dangerous with ice. All of which meant that Nic might actually be able to get home, but it wouldn't be easy or safe.

Worried, feeling cut off from her loved ones and just plain lonely, tears began burning at the back of her eyes. Determined not to start crying again, she sat on the bed and flipped through the channels looking for something light and funny to take her mind off it all.

In a day of unpleasant shocks, seeing her encounter with Monique Dubois on television was a little too much. Then she realized it was a drastically edited version of the encounter complete with a schmaltzy commentary that made her look like a fragile flower and Nic like a conscienceless Lothario.

The remote exploded against the TV screen with a satisfying thwack!

Having paid a small fortune for a first-class ticket, Nic was almost the first one off the plane from St. Louis to O'Hare Airport in Chicago. He checked the flight monitor. The next and last leg of this interminable trip hadn't been cancelled—yet. That gave him ten minutes to get to the gate for the flight to Philadelphia International. He'd spent the day hopping from one airport to the next trying to get to Samantha's side.

As he hurried through the airport, a TV set in a lounge caught Nic's eye. He stopped and stared. The woman on screen bore a sharp resemblance to Samantha. Then he realized it actually was Samantha in her hospital room. Drawn inside he couldn't hear what Samantha was saying because of the noise in the bar. The logo in the bottom corner of the screen belonged to a cable station largely dedicated to celebrity interviews and gossip shows. The camera pulled away and Monique Dubois appeared in the next frame standing next to Samantha.

Close enough to the TV now, Nic could hear Samantha say, "Get out. You aren't allowed in here and I don't need this kind of upset. Leave us alone."

The camera moved in for a close up as tears filled Samantha's lovely, hazel eyes and her lower lip quivered. The film paused and froze on that heartrending image. Nic's heart seemed to stop. She looked brokenhearted.

Then, the image still frozen, there was a voiceover comment. "There you have it. The confession of a self-proclaimed marriage wrecker and her confrontation with the wife of Niccolò Verdini in her hospital room. The couple were married in a Las Vegas ceremony just last July. Their baby girl was born prematurely on March 14th. The film was furnished by an independent reporter. Neither Nic Verdini nor his wife could be reached for comment. But the look on Samantha Verdini's face sort of says it all, doesn't it?"

Nic sank down on a bar stool. She had to believe it. The anguish on her face did, indeed, say it all. He cursed the reputation he'd cultivated in the beginning of his career to garner publicity. Mistakes, he supposed, always came back to haunt you. Today, it seemed, they'd come back to haunt Samantha.

"Hey, pal, you going to just sit there breaking my stirrers or are you going to order something?" a disgruntled voice said from what seemed to be far away.

Nic focused on his hand. He had, indeed, picked up

several plastic stirrers and broken them in half. "Sorry," he muttered, and stood. As he did, he caught sight of the clock behind the bartender's head. He only had five minutes to get to his gate.

He had to get to Samantha. He had to find a way to make her believe that he'd changed. That she was the only woman for him—the only woman he wanted.

There was no way he was missing that flight.

Flying into Philadelphia was only half the battle for Nic. He arrived safely, but the city was still crippled. The regional rails, buses and subways weren't yet running. Driving was nearly impossible, so the rental agencies were refusing to rent cars until the roads were safe. He finally bribed a taxi driver with a promise to pay triple the cost of the fare.

The taxi pulled in front of the Hospital of the University of Pennsylvania with the famed Children's Hospital of Philadelphia right next door. Being so close to CHOP had made him feel better from the start, knowing that if the baby needed their expertise, it wasn't far away.

It was two in the morning when Nic reached the Silverstein Center. He went immediately to see Samantha, but he was told she was sleeping and that he was not allowed in maternity during the middle of the night. The nurse seemed quite annoyed at him.

Not wanting to cause a disturbance, Nic went instead to feed Nicole. Parents were welcome at any hour in the ICN since preemies needed to be fed often and also needed to bond with their parents. He was helpless to stop the smile that formed on his lips when he saw her again. He had not revised his opinion. She was perfect. Too small, of course, but she'd grow.

"Is it time to feed her?" he asked Nicole's primary nurse.

"You're just in time," she assured him.

Nicole was a strong feeder and, in no time, she'd finished the odd-looking little bottle. But Nic wasn't ready to give her up. So he just held his tiny daughter, looking at her finely drawn features. He traced her shell-like ears, then her rosebud lips. He let her wrap her perfect little fingers around his pinky. He'd been right. She was perfection.

"You are gaining weight so quickly. You will soon be allowed to go home. I pray I am still welcome to go with you, *mia piccolo*," he murmured, knowing Nicole preferred low, quiet tones. "You are Papa's little one. You must never forget that. I love you so much. And I love your mama. I hope she knows that. Your papa has not always lived a life to be proud of. I thought it would hurt no one, but now I see how wrong I was. Always, now, the worst is expected of me, and it hurts your mama.

"What a fool I was to go off in a huff. Especially to return to a life I no longer wanted. If she refuses to believe me about Monique, I will lose everything that matters to me."

Samantha's voice broke the silence. "Why on earth would you think you've lost me? Haven't you learned not to believe everything you read?"

Nic looked up. Tears fell from Samantha's lovely

eyes. She looked no different than she had on the television set in Chicago. "*Cara,* again, you cry because I have caused you sadness."

She wiped her eyes and smiled. "No. I'm crying because my hormones are bouncing all over the place. And because of how unfairly you're being treated."

Stunned. Thankful. More in love than ever, Nic held out his free arm and Sam went to him. She sank down next to him in the love seat. Her nearness fed his hungry soul and he looped his arm around her shoulders, pulling her closer. His wife and his daughter in his arms. Nothing in his life had ever felt so good.

"You cannot tell me you never, for one moment, doubted me."

She shook her head. "I did. For a while. But only because of something you said the night Nicole was born. You apologized for what you'd done to me while you were back on the circuit. It made me wonder."

"I meant the worry I caused you. I thought you understood."

She nodded. "I did, but it was pretty odd wording. Remember, it confused me? I tried to call you as soon as I could. I just wanted to hear you tell me it was a lie. I couldn't find you."

The least he could do was let her hear the words. "It was a lie. I tried to call you to tell you so, but you didn't answer your phone. Now I know lines were down all over the east.

"The worst part of the trip wasn't the cancelled flights or the closed airports. In the airport in Chicago,

I saw a bit of the interview you gave. I was sure you believed them. You looked as if your heart had broken."

She groaned. "I saw it, too. I didn't exactly give them an interview. They were hiding in my room when I got back from feeding Nicole. I started crying because she'd given herself away. She said you'd carried her off an elevator and down the hall to your room. I knew then that there wasn't a word of truth to any of what she'd said. A professional wrestler would have had trouble carrying her." Sam gave a watery chuckle. "I was so relieved and so upset for you that I started crying. I wish I understood why that woman would turn up suddenly to say those awful things to hurt you."

"I, too, have been trying to understand it. I cannot."

They sat silent, each thinking—still trying to figure out the motive. But Sam's thoughts took another turn. "Something else was odd, Nic," she said, sitting up and turning toward him. "When the reporter realized I wasn't giving him what he wanted, he asked for my comment on information he had on our marriage. He said he'd learned it wasn't real. That we'd only gotten married so you could still inherit the money from your grandfather's estate. I knew you wouldn't have told anyone about our bar—" She grinned. "Our deal."

The charge nurse tapped on the window before he could comment and entered the little anteroom. "Mr. and Mrs. Verdini, we wouldn't normally do this, but there's a call coming in on the switchboard from Italy. She asked for either one of you. The operator says it's an older woman who sounds very upset."

Nonna. He wondered if something was wrong. They decided to take the call in Samantha's room. Nic reluctantly parted with Nicole and hand in hand, unable to let go of each other, he and Samantha made their way to the room. The phone was already ringing when they opened the door.

Samantha lifted the phone and he bent down to listen. "This is Nonna, Samantha," his grandmother said in their native language.

"I am here as well," he told her.

"Oh, Niccolò, I called to warn you. To warn you both. I have tried to call everyone for hours. I have been so worried. Gina has been mischief making. Your father caught her speaking with a reporter telling lies about you. She confessed to listening on the extension when I spoke with you, Niccolò."

"Now we know who was telling tales."

"She decided to try to destroy your marriage, thinking she had a chance to gain the rest of your share of the estate. She found that horrid woman Niccolò had with him when he was so badly hurt in that race in New York. Gina paid her to pretend Niccolò is having an affair with her. I wanted you to know so you wouldn't be fooled, Samantha. Niccolò loves you greatly."

Samantha smiled. "I know."

"It is all fine, Nonna," Nic told her. "Samantha has great faith in me. Faith I am not sure I have earned, but I am humbled by her trust in me."

They hung up after reporting on the progress Nicole had made in the last few days. Nic took Samantha's hand, pulling her up from the bed and into his arms. "Perhaps we should strike a new bargain."

"Bargain?" she asked, and looked up at him, a teasing light in her lovely eyes. "I thought you never wanted to hear that word again."

"I have changed my mind since it was our bargain that has given me so much. This would be a bargain to keep our little family—and any other additions that may come to us—together forever."

"It's a deal," she whispered, and they sealed their bargain with a kiss.

\* \* \* \* \*

**Every Life Has More
Than One Chapter**

Award-winning author, Stevi Mittman, delivers
another hysterical mystery, featuring Teddi Bayer,
an irrepressible heroine, and her to-die-for hero,
Detective Drew Scoones. After all, life on Long
Island can be murder!

*Turn the page for a sneak peek
at the warm and funny fourth book,
WHOSE NUMBER IS UP, ANYWAY?,
in the Teddi Bayer series,
by STEVI MITTMAN.
On sale August 7.*

"Before redecorating a room, I always advise my clients to empty it of everything but one chair. Then I suggest they move that chair from place to place, sitting in it, until the placement feels right. Trust your instincts when deciding on furniture placement. Your room should "feel right."

—TipsFromTeddi.com

**Gut** feelings. You know, that gnawing in the pit of your stomach that warns you that you are about to do the absolute stupidest thing you could do? Something that will ruin life as you know it?

I've got one now, standing at the butcher counter in King Kullen, the grocery store in the same strip mall as L.I. Lanes, the bowling alley-cum-billiard parlor I'm in the process of redecorating for its "Grand Opening."

I realize being in the wrong supermarket probably doesn't sound exactly dire to you, but you aren't the one buying your father a brisket at a store your mother will somehow know isn't Waldbaum's.

And then, June Bayer isn't your mother.

The woman behind the counter has agreed to go into the freezer to find a brisket for me, since there aren't any in the case. There are packages of pork tenderloin, piles of spare ribs and rolls of sausage, but no briskets.

Warning Number Two, right? I should be so out of here.

But no, I'm still in the same spot when she comes back out, brisketless, her face ashen. She opens her mouth as if she is going to scream, but only a gurgle comes out.

And then she pinballs out from behind the counter, knocking bottles of Peter Luger Steak Sauce to the floor on her way, now hitting the tower of cans at the end of the prepared foods aisle and sending them sprawling, now making her way down the aisle, careening from side to side as she goes.

Finally, from a distance, I hear her shout, "He's deeeeeaaaad! Joey's deeeeaaaad."

My first thought is, *You should always trust your gut.*

My second thought is that, now, somehow, my mother will know I was in King Kullen. For weeks, I will have to hear "What did you expect?" as though whenever you go to King Kullen someone turns up dead. And if the detective investigating the case turns out to be Detective Drew Scoones…well, I'll never hear the end of that from her, either.

She still suspects I murdered the guy who was found dead on my doorstep last Halloween just to get Drew back into my life.

Several people head for the butcher's freezer and I position myself to block them. If there's one thing I've learned from finding people dead—and the guy on my doorstep wasn't the first one—it's that the police get very testy when you mess with their murder scenes.

"You can't go in there until the police get here," I say, stationing myself at the end of the butcher's counter and in front of the Employees Only door, acting as if I'm some sort of authority. "You'll contaminate the evidence if it turns out to be murder."

Shouts and chaos. You'd think I'd know better than to throw the word *murder* around. Cell phones are flipping open and tongues are wagging.

I amend my statement quickly. "Which, of course, it probably isn't. Murder, I mean. People die all the time, and it's not always in hospitals or their own beds, or..." I babble when I'm nervous, and the idea of someone dead on the other side of the freezer door makes me very nervous.

So does the idea of seeing Drew Scoones again. Drew and I have this on-again, off-again sort of thing... that I kind of turned off.

Who knew he'd take it so personally when he tried to get serious and I responded by saying we could talk about *us* tomorrow—and then caught a plane to my parents' condo in Boca the next day? In July. In the middle of a job.

For some crazy reason, he took that to mean that I was avoiding him and the subject of *us*.

That was three months ago. I haven't seen him since.

The manager, who identifies himself and points to his nameplate in case I don't believe him, says he has to go into *his cooler.* "Maybe Joey's not dead," he says. "Maybe he can be saved and you're letting him die in there. Did you ever think of that?"

In fact, I hadn't. But I had thought that the murderer might try to go back in to make sure his tracks were covered, so I say that I will go in and check.

Which means that the manager and I couple up and go in together while everyone pushes against the doorway to peer in, erasing any chance of finding clean prints on that Employee Only door.

I expect to find carcasses of dead animals hanging from hooks and maybe Joey hanging from one, too. I think it's going to be very creepy and I steel myself, only to find a rather benign series of shelves with large slabs of meat laid out carefully on them, along with boxes and boxes marked simply Chicken.

Nothing scary here, unless you count the body of a middle-aged man with graying hair sprawled faceup on the floor. His eyes are wide-open and unblinking. His shirt is stiff. His pants are stiff. His body is stiff. And his expression—you should forgive the pun—is frozen. Bill-the-manager crosses himself and stands mute while I pronounce the guy dead in a sort of *happy now?* tone.

"We should not be in here," I say, and he nods his head emphatically and helps me push people out of the doorway just in time to hear the police sirens and see the cop cars pull up outside the big store windows.

Bobbie Lyons, my partner in Teddi Bayer Interior

Designs—and also my neighbor, my best friend and my private fashion police—and Mark, our carpenter—and my dog sitter, confidant and ego booster—rush in from next door. They beat the cops by a half step and shout out my name. People point in my direction.

After all the publicity that followed the unfortunate incident during which I shot my ex-husband, Rio Gallo, and then the subsequent murder of my first client—which I solved, I might add—it seems like the whole world, or at least all of Long Island, knows who I am.

Mark asks if I'm all right. Did I remember to mention that the man is drop-dead-gorgeous-but-a-decade-too-young-for-me-yet-too-old-for-my-daughter-thank-god? I don't get a chance to answer him because the police are quickly closing in on the store manager and me.

"The woman—" I begin telling the police. Then I have to pause for the manager to fill in her name, which he does: *Fran.*

I continue. "Right. Fran. Fran went into the freezer to get a brisket. A moment later she came out and screamed that Joey was dead. So I'd say she was the one who discovered the body."

"And you are…" the cop asks me. It comes out a bit like, who do I *think* I am, rather than, who am I, really?

"An innocent bystander," Bobbie, hair perfect, make-up just right, says, carefully placing her body between the cop and me.

"And she was just leaving," Mark adds. They each take one of my arms.

Fran comes into the inner circle surrounding the cops. In case it isn't obvious from the hairnet and blood-stained white apron with *Fran* embroidered on it, I explain that she was the butcher who was going for the brisket. Mark and Bobbie take that as a signal that I've done my job and they can now get me out of there. They twist around, with me in the middle, as if we're a Rockettes line, until we are facing away from the butcher counter. They've managed to propel me a few steps toward the exit when disaster—in the form of a Mazda RX7 pulling up at the loading curb—strikes.

Mark's grip on my arm tightens like a vise. "Too late," he says.

Bobbie's expletive is unprintable. "Maybe there's a back door," she suggests, but Mark is right. It's too late.

I've laid my eyes on Detective Scoones. And while my gut is trying to warn me that my heart shouldn't go there, regions farther south are melting at just the sight of him.

"Walk," Bobbie orders me.

And I try to. Really.

*Walk,* I tell my feet. *Just put one foot in front of the other.*

I can do this because I know, in my heart of hearts, that if Drew Scoones was still interested in me, he'd have gotten in touch with me after I returned from Boca. And he didn't.

Since he's a detective, Drew doesn't have to wear one of those dark blue Nassau County Police uniforms. Instead, he's got on jeans, a tight-fitting T-shirt and a tweed sports jacket. If you think that sounds good, you should see him. Chiseled features, cleft chin, brown hair that's naturally a little sandy in the front, a smile that… Well, that doesn't matter. He isn't smiling now.

He walks up to me, tucks his sunglasses into his breast pocket and looks me over from head to toe.

"Well, if it isn't Miss Cut and Run," he says. "Aren't you supposed to be somewhere in Florida or something?" He looks at Mark accusingly, as if he'd been covering for me when he'd told Drew I was gone.

"Detective Scoones?" one of the uniforms says. "The stiff's in the cooler and the woman who found him is over there." He jerks his head in Fran's direction.

Drew continues to stare at me.

You know, how when you were young, your mother always told you to wear clean underwear in case you were in an accident? And how, a little further on, she told you not to go out in hair rollers because you never knew who you might see—or who might see you? And how now your best friend says she wouldn't be caught dead without makeup and suggests you shouldn't either?

Okay, today, *finally,* in my overalls and Converse sneakers, I get it.

I brush my hair out of my eyes. "Well, I'm back," I say. As if he hasn't known my exact whereabouts. The man is a detective, for heaven's sake. "Been back a while."

Bobbie has watched the exchange and apparently decided she's given Drew all the time he deserves. "And we've got work to do, so…" she says, grabbing my arm and giving Drew a little two-fingered wave goodbye.

As I back up a foot or two, the store manager sees his chance and places himself in front of Drew, trying to get his attention. Maybe what makes Drew such a good detective is his ability to focus.

Only, what he's focusing on is me.

"Phone broken? Carrier pigeon died?" he asks me, taking in Fran, the manager, the meat counter and that Employees Only door, all without taking his eyes off me.

Mark tries to break the spell. "We've got work to do there, you've got work to do here, Scoones," Mark says to him, gesturing toward next door. "So it's back to the alley for us."

Drew's lip twitches. "You working the alley now?" he says.

"If you'd like to follow me," Bill-the-manager, clearly exasperated, says to Drew—who doesn't respond. It's as if waiting for my answer is all he has to do.

So, fine. "You knew I was back," I say.

The man has known my whereabouts every hour of the day for as long as I've known him. And my mother's not the only one who won't buy that he "just happened" to answer this particular call. In fact, I'm willing to bet my children's lunch money that he's taken every call within ten miles of my home since the day I got back.

And now he's gotten lucky.

"*You* could have called *me*," I say.

"You're the one who said *tomorrow* for our talk and then flew the coop, chickie," he says. "I figured the ball was in your court."

"Detective?" the uniform says. "There's something you ought to see in here."

Drew gives me a look that amounts to *in or out?*

He could be talking about the investigation, or about our relationship.

Bobbie tries to steer me away. Mark's fists are balled. Drew waits me out, knowing I won't be able to resist what might be a murder investigation.

Finally he turns and heads for the cooler.

And, like a puppy dog, I follow.

Bobbie grabs the back of my shirt and pulls me to a halt.

"I'm just going to show him something," I say, yanking away.

"Yeah," Bobbie says, pointedly looking at the buttons on my blouse. The two at breast level have popped. "That's what I'm afraid of."

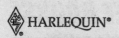

# American ROMANCE®

## Get to the Heart of a Texas Family

### WITH

# THE RANCHER NEXT DOOR
by

# Cathy Gillen Thacker

**She'll Run The Ranch—And Her Life—Her Way!**

On her alpaca ranch in Texas, Rebecca encounters
constant interference from Trevor McCabe, the
bossy rancher next door. Rebecca becomes very
friendly with Vince Owen, her other neighbor and
Trevor's archrival from college. Trevor's problem
is convincing Rebecca that he is on her side, and
aware of Vince's ulterior motives. But Trevor has
fallen for her in the process....

### On sale July 2007

# REQUEST YOUR FREE BOOKS!
## 2 FREE NOVELS PLUS 2 FREE GIFTS!

# SPECIAL EDITION®
### Life, Love and Family!

**YES!** Please send me 2 FREE Silhouette Special Edition® novels and my 2 FREE gifts. After receiving them, if I don't wish to receive any more books, I can return the shipping statement marked "cancel." If I don't cancel, I will receive 6 brand-new novels every month and be billed just $4.24 per book in the U.S., or $4.99 per book in Canada, plus 25¢ shipping and handling per book and applicable taxes, if any*. That's a savings of at least 15% off the cover price! I understand that accepting the 2 free books and gifts places me under no obligation to buy anything. I can always return a shipment and cancel at any time. Even if I never buy another book from Silhouette, the two free books and gifts are mine to keep forever.          235 SDN EEYU  335 SDN EEY6

| | | |
|---|---|---|
| Name | (PLEASE PRINT) | |
| Address | | Apt. |
| City | State/Prov. | Zip/Postal Code |

Signature (if under 18, a parent or guardian must sign)

### Mail to the Silhouette Reader Service™:
**IN U.S.A.:** P.O. Box 1867, Buffalo, NY 14240-1867
**IN CANADA:** P.O. Box 609, Fort Erie, Ontario L2A 5X3

Not valid to current Silhouette Special Edition subscribers.

**Want to try two free books from another line?**
**Call 1-800-873-8635 or visit www.morefreebooks.com.**

* Terms and prices subject to change without notice. NY residents add applicable sales tax. Canadian residents will be charged applicable provincial taxes and GST. This offer is limited to one order per household. All orders subject to approval. Credit or debit balances in a customer's account(s) may be offset by any other outstanding balance owed by or to the customer. Please allow 4 to 6 weeks for delivery.

**Your Privacy:** Silhouette is committed to protecting your privacy. Our Privacy Policy is available online at www.eHarlequin.com or upon request from the Reader Service. From time to time we make our lists of customers available to reputable firms who may have a product or service of interest to you. If you would prefer we not share your name and address, please check here. ☐

SSE07

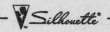

# SPECIAL EDITION™

### Look for

# THE BILLIONAIRE NEXT DOOR

## by *Jessica Bird*

For Wall Street hotshot Sean O'Banyon, going home to south Boston brought back bad memories. But Lizzie Bond, his father's sweet, girl-next-door caretaker, was there to ease the pain. It was instant attraction—until Sean found out she was named sole heir, and wondered what her motives really were....

# THE O'BANYON BROTHERS

**On sale August 2007.**

# COMING NEXT MONTH

**#1843 PAGING DR. RIGHT—Stella Bagwell**
*Montana Mavericks: Striking It Rich*
Mia Smith came to Thunder Canyon Resort for some peace and quiet, but with her recent inheritance, other guests took her for a wealthy socialite and wouldn't leave her be. At least she found comfort with the resort's handsome staff doctor Marshall Cates, but would her painful past and humble beginnings nip their budding romance?

**#1844 THE BILLIONAIRE NEXT DOOR—Jessica Bird**
*The O'Banyon Brothers*
For Wall Street hot shot Sean O'Banyon, going home to South Boston after his abusive father's death brought back miserable memories. But Lizzie Bond, his father's sweet, girl-next-door caretaker, was there to ease the pain. It was instant attraction—and then Sean found out she was named sole heir, and he began to wonder what her motives really were....

**#1845 REMODELING THE BACHELOR—Marie Ferrarella**
*The Sons of Lily Moreau*
Son of a famous, though flighty artist, Philippe Zabelle had grown up to be a set-in-his-ways bachelor. Yet when the successful software developer hired J. D. Wyatt to do some home repairs, something clicked. J.D. was a single mother with a flair for fixing anything... even Philippe's long-broken heart.

**#1846 THE COWBOY AND THE CEO—Christine Wenger**
She was city. He was country. But on a trip to a Wyoming ranch that made disabled children's dreams come true, driven business owner Susan Collins fell hard for caring cowboy Clint Skully. Having been left at the altar once before, would Clint risk the farm on love this time around?

**#1847 ACCIDENTALLY EXPECTING—Michelle Celmer**
In one corner, attorney Miranda Reed, who wrote the definitive guide to divorce and the modern woman. In the other, Zackery Jameson, staunch supporter of traditional family values. When these polar opposites sparred on a radio talk show, neither yielded any ground. So how did it come to pass that Miranda was now expecting Zack's baby?

**#1848 A FAMILY PRACTICE—Gayle Kasper**
After personal tragedy struck, Dr. Luke Phillips took off on a road trip. But when he crashed his motorcycle in the Arizona desert, it was local holistic healer Mariah Cade who got him to stop running. Whether it was in her tender touch or her gentle way with her daughter, Mariah was the miracle cure for all that ailed the good doctor.